Cary Redmond Short Story Anthologies

When Cary Met the Good Guys
Dates, Dinners, and Other Disasters
Witches and Weavers and Ghosts, Oh Boy
A Very Cary Holiday

A VERY CARY HOLIDAY

A CARY REDMOND SHORT STORY ANTHOLOGY

KAT SIMONS

T&D PUBLISHING

A VERY CARY HOLIDAY

CONTENTS

*For my family
And for all our wonderful holidays, both past and future…*

INTRODUCTION

Holiday stories have their own special flavor, and when they're Cary Redmond stories, they also have Trouble. I love holiday fiction, but when I was writing the stories in this collection, I didn't start off thinking, "I will write a holiday story."

Especially the first one, *Cary and the Cursed Jack-O'-Lantern*. It was October when I wrote that, and I was thinking about Halloween, but I hadn't necessarily intended on writing a holiday story. Which is probably why that jack-o'-lantern is…the way it is.

Then came a Christmas story. And, of course, it couldn't be a typical Christmas story, because this is Cary's world. But *Cary Holiday* (get it? Happy Holiday? *grin*) was really fun for me to write because it tapped into something I go through every time I try to take time off. I suspect this is a problem for all of us who work a lot. That first day or so, when you've been so busy, and you just do not know how to relax? Yeah, I related a lot to that restless energy. Take that and a little Christmas tree twist, and *that's* a Cary Christmas.

After I had two holiday stories, as I was putting together a different Cary Redmond collection, I realized it would be fun to write *more* holiday stories with Cary. And as it was rolling into February, I figured why not a Valentine's Day story. Except, honestly, I've never really liked Valentine's Day. I know, I know. I write Romance novels, how can I *not* like Valentine's Day? But I don't. (There might be a little too much of me in Lucy's screed against the holiday.) So instead of Valentine's Day, I absconded with a perfect idea created by the indomitable Leslie Knope of *Parks and Recreation*. Galentine's Day! For Cary and her friends (especially Lucy—you'll see), this was the perfect alternative. The Trouble was just a bonus.

Next came a St. Patrick's Day story. And as I'm writing this introduction *on* St. Patrick's Day, I'm going to take that as good luck. Some readers may know I'm married to an Irishman (we met while I was in graduate school in Dublin), and there's nothing I like better than taking "traditional" Irish tropes and turning them on their heads. Plus, I had the perfect side character for this story—a literal leprechaun! Technically, *Cary's Leprechaun Troubles* could also be thought of as one of the origin stories when Cary first meets one of the important characters in her life, in this case Tom the leprechaun. And honestly, any excuse to put Tom and Jaxer in the same place at the same time is really hard to resist.

Finally, I was hunting around for a holiday that would fit a final story for the collection. I'm not mad about the summer holidays, except for maybe the Summer Solstice, and it felt like I'd covered a bunch of autumn and winter holidays already. Trying to cram in something like Thanksgiving felt like I'd be leaving half the year out. Then I thought about Beltane. And Angie Jordan. And how much fun it is to write a story with those two getting into trouble. Throw in a bonfire and I had *Cary's Beltane Night Out*.

This last story also introduces an…entity that shows up in my newest paranormal romance series—the Seven Families: Wolf series. This isn't the first time some crossover between Cary's world and the Seven Families world has happened (see *Dinner with the Joneses*), but this isn't quite as obvious a link. Really just a little easter egg for readers who enjoy story crossovers and connections.

I've organized the collection so that the first story starts at the beginning of my (witchy) new year—in October—and the rest continue from there. They don't all take place in the same year of

Cary's life, but they do move through the months in order. I didn't start from the beginning of a calendar year mostly because a witchy new year start felt more appropriate to the Cary series. And, in an interesting twist, that's also the order I wrote them in. That almost never happens!

Each story can be read in any order that suits, though. They are all standalones and happen at various stages in Cary's early career—before the start of her main series in The Trouble with Black Cats and Demons. So no Deacon in any of these, I'm afraid. Now that it occurs to me, though, it might be fun to write a whole collection of Cary *and* Deacon holiday stories. Something to think about…

In the meantime, I hope you enjoy A Very Cary Holiday! And that this book brings you a bit of fun, adventure, magic, and Trouble for your own holidays.

Kat Simons
March 2023

CARY AND THE CURSED JACK-O'-LANTERN

Who knew pumpkins could do that?

Cary Redmond encounters a lot of unusual things in her life as a magical Protector. A cursed Jack-O'-Lantern, however, is new. But since the creepy pumpkin is in her best friend's place of business, Cary is quick to help.

The only problem is she has no idea how to stop a curse. Or a pumpkin. Or, really anything. Getting between bad guys and good guys…she does that all day long. Stopping a deadly pumpkin come to life…not so much.

But Cary is up for the challenge. At least, she hopes so.

Because if she's not, it could cost her her best friend's life.

1

$\mathcal{C}$ary Redmond stared at the carved pumpkin sitting five feet away from her, in the front desk area of her best friend Lucy Evans-Nakada's brand new dojo. The pumpkin was one of those big orange things. The face carved into it was an ordinary assortment of triangles and the jagged cut of a smiling mouth. It looked fresh enough. No rot or decay. And with Halloween just two days away, it was the prefect decoration for Lucy's business.

If the pumpkin wasn't, apparently, alive and cursed.

Lucy gripped Cary's shoulders, looking around her arm at the Jack-O'-Lantern. She was significantly more petit than Cary, which didn't mean she couldn't toss Cary around the dojo without breaking a sweat, but it did mean she couldn't actually look *over* Cary's shoulder while she was hiding behind her. Lucy's curly red hair was piled onto her head in a tight bun, little curls escaping to frame her pretty, heart-shaped face. Her brown eyes were wide as she stared at the Jack-O'-Lantern.

"You're sure you saw it do something?" Cary asked, turning her attention back to the pumpkin.

The face carved into it picked that moment to move, its triangle eyes narrowing a little, and a weird cross between a moan and a sawing sound came from the open gap of its mouth.

"See," Lucy said in her high, sweet, little girl voice, "I told you it was alive." Her grip tightened on Cary's shoulders.

The pumpkin had definitely moved in a way that most pumpkins really didn't.

"How long has it been doing that?" Cary asked. She leaned toward the pumpkin then hurriedly straightened away from it when its mouth snapped open and closed.

"It just started before I called you," Lucy said.

The pumpkin jumped forward, a move so sudden and unexpected both Lucy and Cary screeched and stumbled back a few steps. Cary put up an arm to keep Lucy safe behind her.

"Ew," Cary said. "But why did you call me instead of Angie? Angie is the witch. She can actually do something about that thing."

Doing something about a cursed pumpkin was outside Cary's purview. Her skills were strictly defensive. A cursed and moving pumpkin seemed to call for skills of a more offensive nature.

"I *did* call Angie," Lucy said. "She's on a job, reading for one of her rich clients at their house and couldn't get away quickly. She'll be here soon."

"Then why did you call me?"

"So you can keep me safe from that thing until Angie shows up."

"Ah," Cary said. "Well, that's fair enough."

Cary was a magical Protector, a job she'd been tricked into a couple of years ago, but it paid, so she'd gone with it. And it turned out she was pretty good at getting between bad guys and good guys to keep the good guys safe. To be fair, it didn't require an awful lot of specialized skills. Not like the years of training Lucy had needed to earn all her various blackbelts and martial arts skills. Cary just needed the ability to jump into the middle of situations most people ran away from, and then freezing there when confronted with scary things. So long as she was protecting someone from those scary things, her magic worked and her charge was safe. She was a walking, talking Kevlar vest. And her "Kevlar" worked against magic.

Which was good when faced with a living Jack-O'-Lantern.

The pumpkin lurched toward them another few inches. Its jagged mouth moved and a mumbling sound emerged, like it was trying to say something.

Gross.

"How the hell did you end up with a living Jack-O'-Lantern?" Cary asked.

"I have no idea," Lucy said.

"Did you carve it?"

"Not that thing. If I'd carved it, it wouldn't be jumping around."

The pumpkin lurched forward again, and they both screeched.

"Are you sure?" Cary asked. "Did you carve any pumpkins? Maybe you did this on accident?"

Lucy made a snorting noise. "I don't go around accidentally creating cursed pumpkins," she said, sounding indignant. "I'm not the magical one in our group."

Technically, Cary wasn't magical either, except for the magic her bosses gave her as a Protector, but since Lucy didn't even have that, her point was valid.

"But did you carve any pumpkins?" Cary asked again.

"Sure. One. But it didn't have that basic face. Mine was much more elaborate. My dad wouldn't have it any other way."

Cary smiled at that. One of Lucy's fathers had done a little competitive pumpkin carving in his youth before taking off to be a fulltime surfer in Hawaii, where he'd met Lucy's other father. They both still happily lived in Kaneohe on Oahu. Lucy had moved to Portland, Oregon a few years ago, using the excuse that it was a less expensive place to open her own dojo. She was still close with her fathers, but Cary suspected Lucy liked the independence of living off the island.

Cary couldn't blame her. She loved her own parents, but the three hour drive between her home and theirs was…useful.

"Okay," Cary said, "so not your pumpkin. Was it a gift? Did someone bring it to you?"

"Not that I noticed." She paused to look around. "And my beautiful pumpkin is definitely missing. Bastards."

"It's really cute when you curse with your little voice," Cary commented.

"And for that crack, you owe me a drink. Later. When we survive the deadly pumpkin."

"Are we sure it's deadly?" Cary asked, trying to lean closer to the pumpkin to look at it better while at the same time leaning away from it because a moving Jack-O'-Lantern was gross.

"It's moving and trying to talk. I'm not taking any chances."

"Could it just be a trick?" Cary said, wondering out loud. "Like a joke someone is playing on you, and it's not really dangerous?"

"Are your powers working?" Lucy countered.

Actually, Cary couldn't tell. She couldn't feel her magic. Whatever her bosses had given her, it just flowed through her when she needed it, but she didn't really sense it or have any control over it. Which was pretty irritating, but according to her faery mentor, Jaxer, it was because she was a mundane human outside of the Protector magic. If she'd had some of her own supernatural skills before getting tricked into this job, she'd have had a better sense of the Protector magic she channeled.

At least that was Jaxer's story.

"I could test it," Cary said. "But it means you'll have to get closer to the pumpkin. If it attacks you, we'll know."

"Gee, that sounds like a wonderful idea," Lucy said, heavy on the sarcasm. With her sweet, high voice, though, the sarcasm just sounded cute.

"Come on. You're the fighter. And if it does attack, I'm protecting you. And we'll know it's actually dangerous."

"Or we could just wait for Angie and let the trained witch take care of it," Lucy said.

"You're going to feel silly if it's just a trick being run by some sort of inner mechanical stuff, like those skeletons you hang on the door that have motion detectors and jump at people when they get close."

Lucy pointed past Cary's arm. "That thing is not made of plastic. And those skeleton tricks don't walk around the front yard after you hang them on the door."

She had a point.

Still.

"You know, it's just a little pumpkin. We could probably just pick it up and put it outside and be done with it," Cary said.

"And endanger some poor innocent cat or dog?" Lucy said. "What if it eats them?"

"Oh, right. No, that would be bad." They'd bonded over their mutual love of animals and the fact that they both dealt with parents nagging them to settle down into a relationship. "Okay, so, what…? We just watch it until Angie arrives?"

"I'm game if you are," Lucy said.

"How long did she say she'd take?"

The pumpkin lurched toward them again, its mouth snapping open and closed. It didn't sound like hollow, soft pumpkin smashing together, though. When the sharp, jagged peaks of its teeth clashed, it sounded like something significantly harder. And more likely to hurt.

"Her client is that rich lady who goes on and on about her dead aunt and the conversations they've been having," Lucy said.

"Angie isn't a medium," Cary stated the obvious. "Why does this lady keep calling her in?"

"Got me. I think she's just using Angie as her therapist."

In a weird way, given Angie read futures for her clients, she probably did do a lot of work similar to a therapist's. "Isn't this the lady that can keep her there half the night?"

"That's the one," Lucy said. "And given how much she pays, I can't blame Angie for keeping her on as a client."

The pumpkin started to moan again. The sound made the hairs on Cary's arm stand up. It was a cross between midnight wind blowing through bare tree branches, and an actual human in pain. It was a very creepy sound. Not least because it was coming from a hollowed out *pumpkin.*

They both watched as the pumpkin's mouth worked, like it was chewing something. Cary could literally see inside it, through its triangle eyes. It was a hollow gourd. It shouldn't be this scary. What was the worst it could do?

It lurched closer, another jump toward them.

And a cockroach crawled out of its eye.

2

"Ew," Cary said, unable to look away from the probably-cursed Jack-O'-Lantern.

"Gross," Lucy said. "I keep my dojo spotless. I don't want roaches in here."

The cockroach that had just crawled out of the pumpkin's triangular eye hole climbed along its face then back toward its mouth. The pumpkin snapped and the roach disappeared into its mouth with a crunching noise as the pumpkin's mouth worked in a chewing motion again.

"Ew," Cary said again.

"Gross," Lucy repeated.

"At least you don't have to worry about the roach getting free in your dojo."

"That doesn't improve the situation," Lucy said. "That pumpkin just ate a cockroach."

"To be fair, it also produced the cockroach," Cary felt compelled to state.

"Still not helping the situation," Lucy said.

"You know, it's doing things to be scary. Like, on purpose."

"Cause it's a scary moving pumpkin. I'm not sure it can do anything else but be scary."

"No, I mean that thing it just did with the roach. That seemed designed to be gross and scary. Why produce a roach from your eye only to eat it?"

"Maybe it was hungry," Lucy suggested.

"Ew. Yeah. But no, what I mean is, this all seems like... I don't know. Like it's a purposeful trick."

"I didn't piss anyone off enough for them to 'trick' me this way," Lucy said.

"You're sure?"

"Yes! Outside of you and Angie and Marianne, I don't hang out with the kind of people capable of that." Lucy gestured to the pumpkin as it lurched toward them some more.

"Marianne and I aren't capable of *that* either," Cary said. Marianne was a weaver—she could do miraculous and magical things with clothe and thread—but those skills didn't extend to cursing gourds. "And Angie believes in that 'do no harm' creed of witches. She wouldn't do this."

"I would have thought this sort of curse or whatever falls under the 'you send it out and it'll come back three times worse' thingy," Lucy said.

"That too."

A noise like breaking bones came from the pumpkin, though how and why Cary couldn't tell. It was like the worst clichés of Halloween all rolled into one weird joke. Except she wasn't betting money anymore that this "joke" was harmless.

"You must have pissed someone off," Cary said.

"Can't imagine who?"

"Who did you rent this shop from?"

Lucy had been forced to move out of her last location because of a rent hike, but this store had come available fortuitously just when she needed it. The rent was perfect. And it was even in a better location than her last dojo, closer to Chinatown.

Only now, while staring down a living Jack-O'-Lantern, did Cary stop to consider just how lucky Lucy's finding this place had been. Maybe too lucky?

"Okay, this is ridiculous," Cary said. "It's a gourd. A hollowed out gourd—"

"That just ate a cockroach," Lucy interrupted.

"It doesn't have hands or feet. How dangerous could it be?"

"Snakes don't have hands or feet either," Lucy said. "They're still super dangerous."

"They have teeth. And strong muscles."

"That has teeth."

"But not strong muscles." Though Cary wasn't absolutely positive about that. The thing was moving around when it shouldn't have been. Still… "I'm just going to pick it up and see what's happening. If this is nothing more than a trick-or-treat trick, we're both going to feel really silly."

"I never feel silly taking precautions. I'm the girl in the horror movie who gets *into* the running car and drives away from the haunted farm. I sure as hell don't go down into the basement."

Cary laughed. "I never thought I was the 'go into the basement to investigate' type either. Guess I was wrong." She took a few steps closer to the pumpkin. Lucy stayed behind her, clinging to her arms.

"You know they have a name for those kinds of characters, right?" Lucy said.

"What is it?"

"Too stupid to live."

"Right." Cary stopped moving toward the pumpkin. "But seriously. It's a gourd."

"Which ate a cockroach."

"You're really stuck on that roach thing, aren't you?"

"Aren't you?" Lucy fairly screeched.

"It's not the grossest or weirdest thing I've seen in the last couple of years," Cary said with a shrug.

That guy possessed by a water spirit that he'd purposefully called into himself so he could take revenge on an ex-girlfriend had easily been the grossest thing she'd seen so far. His skin had turned an unnatural gray color and sloughing off in chunks, his hair dripped with seaweed, and water leaked out of him in strange, unnatural glops. That had been really gross.

A little roach eating paled in comparison.

"I'm just going to get a little closer and see if there's a trick to this thing," Cary said. "Stay behind me and we'll be fine, even if it is cursed."

They inched toward the pumpkin again. It seemed to stare at them, not moving so much anymore, but its mouth was still working, sawing back and forth, reminding Cary a little of the way someone with dentures in might move their mouth around when they didn't have their dentures in. Except this thing still had all its teeth.

Another shrieking moan erupted from the hollows of the pumpkin, making Cary's arm hair stand up again. The piercing sound hurt her ears this time. The closer they got to the pumpkin, the more the thing's mouth moved, and it's outer shell expanded and contracted, like it was breathing.

Or about to explode.

She'd barely formed the thought, when a stream of goo shot from the pumpkin's mouth, right at them. The goo was stringy and a sickly yellow color. It smelled horrible, like an accidentally perforated gut. And when it hit the ground, it burned holes in the wooden floor like acid.

"My floor!" Lucy said in outrage. "Someone's going to pay for that."

"How are you going to explain this to the insurance company? Floor burnt by acid spewing from cursed Jack-O'-Lantern."

Lucy snorted. "Good thing my dad taught me how to do some wood work."

"Henry or Steve?"

"Henry, of course."

"Of course." The surfer dad. He was a fount of useful skills and practical talents, which included starting a number of businesses that he then sold for a profit. Steve's greatest skill was, apparently, making money and managing other people's money. Which Cary thought was also a really useful and practical talent.

"I think maybe we shouldn't get any closer to the pumpkin," Cary said, watching the acid goo smoke. She covered her nose with her hand to block some of the smell. "I had no idea anything that came from a pumpkin could smell that bad."

"It is cursed after all."

"Ha," she said, without any humor. "Uh, is it just me, or does it seem to be…growing?"

"It's not just you. It's getting bigger. That's not good, is it?"

"No. No, it's not."

As the goo spread toward them in a slow, sickly yellow creep, the pumpkin itself seemed to swell. It was like one of those documentaries that sped up the life cycle of a growing plant.

Except in real life.

Without the handy time dilations.

Which was a very scary thing for a hollow gourd to do.

ary started moving backward, Lucy still safely behind her. She was pretty sure the acid-like goo the pumpkin had spewed couldn't get through her shields to reach them, and no matter how big the Jack-O'-Lantern got, they'd be safe. It was what she did after all. What her Protector magic did. Still…

Acid popping goo and a growing pumpkin weren't things she wanted to stand right next to.

"How big do you think it'll get?" Lucy asked when the pumpkin hit the size of a wolfhound.

"No idea."

"Can you stop it?"

"From reaching you? Yes. From growing? No. I'm not even sure how that's possible."

And then it all got worse, because the pumpkin sprouted arms.

"Ew," Cary said.

"Gross," Lucy added.

They took another few steps away from the arm-growing, small-car-sized pumpkin.

"Is it good it still hasn't sprouted feet?" Lucy asked.

"Yeah, no. I'm not sure it needs them."

Sure enough, the thing used its arms to lunge forward, planting its hands on the floor and lifting its still roundish body up, then swinging forward a few feet. It landed in the middle of the yellow goo, which caused it to splatter, some of it landing perilously close to Cary's feet.

She wrinkled her nose at the smell. "I'm so sorry about your front desk area," she said to Lucy.

"My woodworking skills will not fix this. It's gonna cost a fortune. Who's going to pay for this? I'm positive my insurance won't cover supernatural pumpkin attacks."

"We should probably survive the pumpkin attack before we worry about insurance."

"Fair point," Lucy said, her little girl voice squeaking when the pumpkin lunged another foot closer.

It was as tall as Cary now, on its way to being taller, and as wide as an industrial-sized freezer. It stopped its forward lunge when it reached the edge of the goo circle. Cary risked looking down. The goo was piling up against an invisible barrier. Her Protector shields in action. Yay for shields!

The pumpkin's long arms extended, longer than real arms—although what constituted "real" arms for a pumpkin was anyone's guess. They stretched and wove forward toward Cary and Lucy. Vines, like pulsing green veins, bulged long thick orange muscles. Its hands were shaped vaguely like a human's, with five fingers, but more skeletal and with the tips of the fingers covered in hard caps, a little like the stem on its head, but whittled into wickedly sharp points. Its jagged-cut teeth had elongated and gone from pale-orange to a brown, hard surface—which looked like it could actually chew and bite and… hurt. A lot.

The inside no longer seemed hollow, but Cary couldn't see anything beyond darkness. Probably for the best, she thought, when another stream of acid yellow goo shot from its mouth to splatter against her shield.

"That would have hurt," Cary said.

"Ah," Lucy said.

Cary couldn't tell what that meant for sure, but she had a feeling

Lucy had just stepped past the dealing-with-this into the overwhelmed-by-fear stage. She couldn't blame her. The damned pumpkin was still getting bigger, its stemmed cap reaching close to the ceiling now, looming over them so Cary had to look up to see into its triangle eyes. Triangle eyes that now glowed yellow. Like there was a candle inside the Jack-O'-Lantern. The nose glowed yellow, too.

The mouth remained a huge gaping hole of blackness.

A blackness now large enough for Cary to step into and only have to duck a little.

"What now?" Lucy squeaked.

"You stay behind me."

Cary glanced down. Her shields continued holding the goo back, thankfully. The pumpkin's reaching arms swung at the air in front of her but couldn't reach her or Lucy through the Protector magic. So long as Lucy stuck to Cary's back, Cary's magic would continue to work, and all the pumpkin's growing, moaning, acid-spitting efforts couldn't hurt them.

But the stink of it all was making Cary's eyes water. "Let's start to move toward the front door."

"My dojo," Lucy moaned.

"I know, I know. I promise I'll help you clean up this mess when this is all over. But we need to get out of here. I think it's too big to get out the door now, so we can trap it inside and keep watch until Angie arrives."

Boy, she hoped Angie arrived soon.

The biggest drawback to being a magical Protector was that her skills were purely defensive. She had *no* offensive talents or magic or anything. She couldn't even throw a bad guy over her head the way Lucy could—unless they charged her while she was protecting someone and it was necessary. Her magic gave her all the skills she needed to keep people safe in the moment. But they were reactions. Not actions. She couldn't *do* anything to get rid of the pumpkin or remove its curse or anything.

But she could stand between it and Lucy, and the rest of Portland for that matter, if she had to, and for a very long time.

They edged toward the front door, moving carefully to avoid the melted parts of the wooden floor. The pumpkin wobbled around, following their movements with its glowing eyes and making little hopping movements to keep them in view. It reached for them again with its weird arms, but couldn't get past the invisible block of Cary's magic.

Another deep moan emerged from the thing. And then a sound so piercing—a scraping, screeching, ear-splitting dragging sound—Cary had to cover her ears. The room seemed to vibrate with the screech, and for a horrifying moment, Cary thought the vibrations would break the windows at the front of the dojo.

"Stop it," Lucy shouted at the pumpkin.

They'd reached the door, but Cary couldn't concentrate over the shriek. Not enough to work the door handle. The pumpkin's scream was so painfully piercing, she thought her ears might bleed.

Why the hell weren't her powers preventing that?

Realizing that they were and that this would probably be a lot worse without the Protector magic made her wince.

She was trying to find a way to block her ears and still open the front door, as the acid goo piled up against her shield again, and the cursed Jack-O'-Lantern reached for them, swatting its sharp fingers across the air in front of Cary. That would hurt like hell if it got through to her. Though probably not much worse than her exploding head from the creature's screech.

The door vibrated at her back, mostly a wooden structure with a large inset window so people could see in and out, but so the dojo didn't feel like a glass fronted retail space. The wood bulged inward, then out, alternately pressing against Cary's back and moving away. The damn thing was going to burst apart before she remembered how to work the handle. She tried leaning against it, just pushing it with her back and hoping the door magically opened, but then it bulged away from her, leaving her frustrated at not being able to do something so simple.

She needed her hands.

Wincing, she dropped her hands from her ears and reached for the door handle, pushing hard.

The door came off its hinges and flew out onto the sidewalk.

Uhm.

She was pretty sure, even with her powers, she wasn't strong enough to do that. She hadn't applied that much force. Had the pumpkin's screaming done that?

And then Angie through the doorway.

4

"*O*uch," Angie mouthed, covering her ears.

"Understatement," Cary shouted. "Also good to see you. Can you do something about that?" She gestured toward the pumpkin which was pushing up against the ceiling now, its screech causing the whole building to shake dangerous. She covered her own ears again, grateful for the very slight reprieve.

She didn't want to imagine what this would feel like without her Protector magic dampening the sound.

Angie gestured them all outside. "Safer," she said.

Though Cary had to read her lips because she couldn't hear her over the noise.

On the sidewalk, Cary could now see the way the building was starting to bulge at the edges. Oh man, Lucy's insurance really wasn't going to cover this. Maybe they could come up with some excuse?

Angie stepped behind Cary, next to Lucy, putting Cary between herself and the building and the cursed pumpkin. Cary grinned over her shoulder at Angie. The woman was smart, and never hesitated to take advantage of Cary's powers while gearing up to use her own.

Outside, the noise wasn't quite so piercing, though still not comfortable. The orange sides of the pumpkin pushed against the now wide open door. Fortunately, the neighborhood was a relatively quiet business area, at the very edge of the Pearl.

"No apartments above the place," Angie muttered. "I was thinking about this on the way over. I may have to light it up."

"Huh?" Cary said, glancing over her shoulder.

"I've never had to stop a—growing?—growing cursed Jack-O'-Lantern before," Angie said. "Not the type of thing you see every day."

Angie didn't sound particularly surprised by the cursed pumpkin, just acknowledged that it wasn't common. For some reason, the fact that this wasn't common was reassuring to Cary. Unlike Angie, who'd been part of the supernatural community for her entire life, Cary hadn't even known most of this stuff existed a couple of years ago. Frankly, she was still learning what was "normal" in a very not-normal world.

"The only thing I can think to do," Angie continued, "since I don't know who cursed the pumpkin or what magic they used, is to burn the think down."

Lucy moaned. "That's going to destroy my dojo, isn't it?"

Angie gave her a shoulder hug and nodded to the bulge of orange rind pressing through the door. "Sweetie, I think your dojo is already destroyed."

"But, on the bright side," Cary said, "a fire is more likely to be covered by your insurance than a cursed pumpkin."

"True," Lucy said. "So long as the landlord and fire inspectors don't claim I started the fire. And since Angie is about to start the fire…"

"I'm pretty sure I can make it look like an accident after the fact," Angie said, not sounding as certain as she did about cursed pumpkins being unusual.

"Oh boy," Cary muttered.

But the pumpkin was definitely pushing out of the building now. Something had to be done, or that thing would not only shatter the stone structure of the place, it would get loose and start moving around Portland.

That seemed like a bad idea.

"Do what you need to do," Lucy said, sounding sad. "I knew this location and rent were too good to be true anyway."

Cary turned her back on dangerous gourd long enough to give Lucy a hug. Then faced the threat again, easing her two friends back to the very edge of the sidewalk. The street was quiet, it had gotten pretty late and there wasn't much nighttime traffic along this road, but thanks to luck or some wise human instincts, there was even less car and pedestrian traffic than usual. That meant Cary only had to keep Lucy and Angie safe from what happened next.

Whatever that was going to be.

Over her shoulder to Angie, she said, "You might want to get to the magical immolation stuff, because, uh, the walls are bulging."

The stonework was actually moving outward and inward a little, like it was breathing. That didn't bode well for the building's continued existence.

Angie started chanting something under her breath, her normally deep voice dropping to an even deeper register. Because Cary's mentor Jaxer kept pushing her to study and learn everything she could about the supernatural world, Cary tried to catch the language Angie was using. Thanks to some Latin classes in college—to avoid doing a language she might have to speak aloud since she sucked at languages —she recognized what she thought might be some Latin. But since she usually looked at written Latin and hadn't heard it out loud often, she wasn't able to tell exactly what Angie was saying. She was pretty sure she heard *incendere*, but that could be down to the fact she knew Angie was about the burn some pumpkin.

For a very long time, nothing happened but the building continuing to swell dangerously. One of the front windows burst, scattering glass across the sidewalk as more pumpkin hide pressed the resistance of the outer building. Lucy whimpered as a second window shattered. Cary reached back and held her hand but kept her gaze on the building—just in case.

It was morbidly fascinating watching the orange bulging out of the dojo that way. She wouldn't admit that to Lucy, though.

The pumpkin's vine-covered arms reached out through the front door, stretching its creepy sharp fingers toward them. More vines crawled over the outside of the building façade, stabbing into the stonework. The acid goo flowed out the front door like slow moving lava, not in a hurry but relentlessly sizzling all in its path.

The stench rolled out as well, making Cary gage as more windows shattered. The pumpkin's fingers swiped at them, reaching and flexing, the hands now the size of small cars. And its piercing screech continued to make her ears hurt even though they were no longer confined in a small space with it.

She kept waiting for some signs of smoke or flames. And waiting. And waiting.

"Angie," she said after what felt like a reasonable amount of waiting time, "is this going to work or…not?"

Angie was still chanting under her breath. Cary didn't dare look back at her anymore, but she got the impression Angie was also using hand gestures to build her spell. Angie was a multi-talented witch with several skills at her disposal, her psychic talent being her strongest. Her spell-casting was generally pretty strong too, but relied on word-spells and gestures and sometimes potions—unlike wizards which, Cary had learned fairly recently, relied on a sort of internal magic different to a witch's, and they could toss around their magic in a way a witch couldn't. Wizards weren't just the "male" version of a witch. They were a different type of magic wielder all together.

Angie couldn't just throw a ball of flame or an energy bolt at the monster trying to burst out of Lucy's dojo. She had to get the fire started through a different magical process.

One that, from the outside, didn't look like it was working.

The goo reached Cary's shield again, starting to form a little mound in front of them. The monster's screech was reaching a pitch that made Cary's eyes water. And the building looked like it was one push away from splitting open like a…well, an exploded pumpkin. The irony was not lost on her.

She eased her charges back another few steps, so they were almost moving into the—still amazingly empty!—street. The goo followed, the sidewalk hissing and crackling.

And then she saw the first lick of flames. The pumpkin's glowing yellow eye peeked through a hole that had opened near the building's roof, staring at them, but deep inside the glowing depth, Cary spotted a burst of red. Near one of the shattered windows, smoke billowed, and a flash of uneven light changed to actual flames crawling along the orange pumpkin rind pressed against the window.

The cursed Jack-O'-Lantern screamed. Not just the ear-splitting, relentless screech but a howl of denial and pain that literally made the ground shake. Like an earthquake. Cary stumbled and held up her arms to keep Angie and Lucy braced as they bumped into her. The flames grew, punching through orange rind and streaking the shell in black soot.

Cary was a little grossed out to realize the cooking pumpkin actually smelled good. She would never look at roasted vegetables in quite the same way.

The flames spread fast then, growing and engulfing the building in a rush of heat and light. Within moments, everything was burning, even the goo that had spread out onto the sidewalk. The heat was breath-stealing, the light blinding.

Despite the flames flickering toward them, Cary didn't flinch away. She might not have been able to start the fire, but she could protect her friends from it—her particular brand of magic worked against the mundane as well as the magical. Which was convenient when someone tried to shoot or stab her.

But the heat was not comfortable. Checking for cars first, she hurried Angie and Lucy across the street, still keeping between them and the flames.

From the relative safety of the opposite sidewalk, they watched Lucy's dojo burn. Cary winced when the pumpkin's scream reached a high pitched wail and then blackened rind and pumpkin seeds shattered out in an explosion of gourd that would have made the pumpkin chunkin' crowd proud.

Lucy made a choking noise. Cary finally turned away from the destruction to face her friend. Lucy had tears leaking down her cheeks, but her expression was more confused than sad.

"I'd really love to know *why* that happened," she said, her little girl voice deeper than normal. "And who's responsible for putting a cursed Jack-O'-Lantern inside my dojo. Cause whoever it was, we're going to have words about this."

Cary raised her brows at Lucy's tone. She sounded…dangerous.

When they'd first met, Cary had witnessed Lucy tossing around a handful of fully grown men with ease, throwing them like they were rag dolls. They'd attacked her, she was defending herself, but it had not been a fair fight. If they'd wanted to take on Lucy, they'd really needed more than four of them.

Cary almost felt sorry for the stupid ass person who'd gotten on Lucy's bad side.

"Sorry," Angie said. She hugged Lucy to her, but she met Cary's gaze. "Sorry that took so long to get started." She nodded at the building. "I had to build a circle around it first to keep the flames from spreading. Magic fire is just as likely to get out of control as real fire and once it does, there's no stopping it. I didn't want to burn down the neighborhood."

"I'm sure the neighborhood appreciates your caution," Cary said. "I do, too. Thanks. And thanks for coming to help."

Angie grinned. "Anything for my friends." She looked back at the building. "I wish I'd known you'd rented this place, though," she said to Lucy.

"Why? What was wrong with it? I knew the rent was too good."

"Nothing's wrong with the building itself. Just the last tenant was Madame LeRoux, a Vodun priestess."

"Did she put a curse on the building or something?" Cary asked.

"Oh no." Angie waved that away. "She's a lovely woman. She did a great business here catering to tourists looking for 'authentic voodoo gris gris.' She was a bit like me, playing up the stereotypes of her religion to sell stuff. But in real life, she's a nice woman whose real name is Gale Tyler."

"Why isn't she renting this shop anymore?" Cary asked.

"She had to move back to Louisiana to help her brother look after their aging father," Angie said with a shrug.

"What does that have to do with the cursed pumpkin?" Lucy asked.

"Well, her reasons for moving were practical," Angie said, "but she had a few enemies she left behind. There's a rival priest across town who really hated LeRoux. He occasionally sent curses her way." Angie smiled. "She occasionally sent curses back at him."

"I take it LeRoux usually got the best of those exchanges?" Cary said with a little grin. Then winced when she looked over her shoulder at the smoldering remains of the dojo. "Except maybe this time."

"I thought he knew she'd moved," Angie said. "But maybe he'd set this up before she left and forgot to stop the spell. Or couldn't stop it. He's not nearly as skilled as Gale. Plus, he's kind of an ass. He probably didn't care if someone innocent got hurt."

"Someone is going to get hurt," Lucy said with a snarl. "Him."

"No no no," Angie said. "You are not going after that asshole. He's dangerous in a way you can't fight." She gestured to the building. "I'll give Gale a call, let her know what happened. She'll take care of him."

"From Louisiana?" Cary asked, raising her brows.

Angie smiled again. "She might be a nice woman, but she's also a powerful one. Raymond should never have challenged her." She sighed. "Man's gonna wish he'd stuck to selling cars."

"Good," Lucy said, the viciousness in her tone not lessened at all by the sweetness of her voice.

They all turned to look at the burning building.

True to her word, Angie's magical fire didn't spread to the neighboring shops. But it consumed Lucy's dojo completely, leaving a blackened, smoldering pile of brick in its wake.

They stood in silence and hugged Lucy, watching the destruction, which moved faster than a normal fire would have.

As the flames started to die down—Angie promised they'd go out fully and not leave any dangerous hotspots behind that could flare up again—Cary glanced around the street.

"Uhm," she said, "why didn't anyone call the fire department? Or the cops? Or come out to see what was happening?" The total lack of witnesses or traffic or emergency vehicles was a little too complete.

"You're welcome," a deep male voice said from behind a sidewalk tree.

Cary's faery mentor, Jaxer, stepped from behind the tree, grinning at her. He was stupidly handsome with long blond hair, electric blue-green eyes, and sharply angular features that called to mind old world gods. His grin could charm mud, and he always dressed in ways that showed off his muscular physique even when the clothes were inappropriate to the weather—like now, since it was a chilly October night and he was wearing a silk shirt with several of the top buttons opened to show off his chest. Jaxer's greatest magic was glamour—the ability to make others see what he wanted them to see—so she didn't tend to take his looks or his charm too seriously.

She did shiver as his shirt billowed in a cold breeze. How did he not need a coat?

As her mentor, Jaxer was teaching Cary how to be a Protector, helping her when she needed it. He showed up whenever he liked, but was almost always there when she needed him. After the last couple of years—though she wouldn't admit it to him—she'd grown to really like Jaxer and considered him a friend. Even if he was pretty irritating most of the time.

"You're responsible for the quiet street?" she asked, waving a hand vaguely at their peopleless surroundings.

He gave her a shoulder hug and kissed her cheek. She rolled her eyes, which made him grin.

"Yes," he said, "I figured you'd need a little extra help keeping this from spreading."

"Thank you," Cary said, meaning it.

"Anything for you, love," he said with a grin that was a lot more authentic this time. Then he looked at Lucy, who was staring at him with wide eyes. "I'm so sorry about your place, though," he said.

"Uh huh," Lucy mumbled around her slack mouth.

Cary realized Lucy hadn't met Jaxer before this, though he floated in and out of Cary's life all the time. She was a little surprised they hadn't met, but given Lucy's stunned expression, Cary figured introductions were in order.

Lucy made an attempt to shake Jaxer's proffered hand, but she couldn't drag her gaze from his face.

Cary bit back a smile.

"You look like you could use a drink," Jaxer said to Lucy, slinging an arm around her shoulder. "Don't worry about your place. I'll talk to the insurance people. They'll rebuild for you, and it won't cost you anything. Terrible thing a gas leak and a fire, isn't it? Lucky no one was there to get hurt."

"Uh huh," Lucy said.

Cary stopped hiding her smile as Jaxer walked Lucy up the road, continuing to spin the story he'd tell the authorities to make sure this all turned out well and no one realized exactly what had happened. Given his glamour, Cary didn't doubt for a minute he'd be able to pull off getting Lucy's business back up and running in no time.

"He's very good at cleaning up after things," she said to Angie.

"Is he?" Angie asked.

"Does it all the time for me," Cary said with a nod.

Angie frowned a little. Then shook her head and said, "I don't know about you, but I could use a drink, too. What do you say?"

"So long as it doesn't have pumpkin in it," Cary said with feeling, glancing one last time at the smoking pile of bricks that had been Lucy's dojo.

They turned to follow Jaxer and Lucy to the Irish pub at the top of the road.

"That's gonna be tricky this time of year," Angie said. "Everything has pumpkin in it."

Cary winced. Oh boy.

CARY HOLIDAYS

A quiet holiday shouldn't be too much to ask...

Unless of course your name is Cary Redmond and your job title is Magical Protector. But in the days leading up to Christmas, in her second year as a Protector, Cary might just get the quiet time off she hopes for.

Nothing to do but watch Christmas movies, drink Christmas coffee, maybe even decorate for the season. No shapeshifter trouble. No vampires up to no good. No demons popping in to threaten death. Just peace and quiet. Lots and lots of quiet.

Until, of course, her new Christmas tree reveals a surprising complication...

That is anything but peaceful.

$\mathcal{C}$ary Redmond lifted her steaming mug of peppermint coffee to her nose and breathed in deeply. The house was quiet, blessedly quiet. The dogs were asleep on their beds under her living room bay window after their morning stomp around the backyard. Her bosses had promised she wouldn't be needed for at least the next few days. Her faery mentor "warned" her he had business elsewhere so she wouldn't see him for a few days. Her parents had already texted to say they were safely ensconced in her sister's house in New York. It was a gloriously cold and bright sunny day.

And she had nothing to do but sit around watching Christmas movies and reading Christmas novels and enjoying some well-earned peace.

It had been a hell of a couple of years. Since being tricked into this job as a magical Protector, she'd felt like she'd barely had time for a breath. When she wasn't running around at her bosses' biding to save good guys from bad guys, she was deep in her books learning about... well, everything. She hadn't even known the supernatural world existed before this job. Now she had all this stuff she needed to learn to catch up. And there never seemed enough time.

She cast a guilty look up at her ceiling. With the break, and a quiet

Christmas ahead of her, she probably should get a little more studying in. Her finished attic contained her library and office—safely hidden so when her parents came to visit, they didn't stumble on books with titles like *Updated Phylogeny Classifications for Demons from Realms B and X* and *Current Theory Pertaining to the Magical Arts in Post-Modern Wizardry*. Her parents thought she was a research assistant for a former professor who wrote popular science books. They didn't need to know about her new job.

And with them safely on the opposite side of the country visiting her sister, Cary was free to enjoy the holiday without the constant dread that her parents would drive the three hours from the coast to visit her as a Christmas "surprise" only to have them knock while her bosses were here sending her out to save someone, or her ridiculously handsome faery mentor was here. She wasn't sure her parents would know what to say to the North American Fae who were her bosses—especially since they very obviously didn't look human. But she was *certain* her mother would get the wrong idea about Jaxer. Her mentor was too vain to show her mother anything less than his ridiculously gorgeous persona, and her mother would definitely decide Jaxer would make a good son-in-law.

Little did she know.

For now, though, Cary didn't have to worry about any of that. No mentors, bosses, or parents to worry about. And she could work on studying later. After all, she had days to herself. Finally!

She settled deeper into her overstuffed couch, savoring her sweetened, milky peppermint coffee. This was the life. Quiet. Peaceful. No noise. No wizards throwing magic at her. No vampires causing trouble. No demons. No witches or shapeshifters attacking anyone. No ordinary assholes with guns trying to kill people. No angry gnomes causing a ruckus. No chaos. No mayhem.

Nothing but glorious peace.

She closed her eyes to listen to the quiet. The sounds of her three dogs snuffling in their sleep made her smile. Her golden Labrador, Buck, who was actually a demon dog, made a deep puttering sound that was almost a snore. Pickles, her foo lion living as a basset hound, made a little huff every few moments but was otherwise breathing quietly. Fred, the mundane terrier-collie mix, whined and his kicking paws scrapped the floor, as if he was chasing squirrels in his sleep. Fred was all about the chase. She hoped he never caught that squirrel. That would be a perfect dream for Fred.

She opened her eyes to contemplate the stack of DVDs and books on her coffee table. Movie first. *Die Hard* because it was Christmas time and she needed a good Christmas movie. Then maybe one of the novels—a fluffy holiday romance or a fast-paced holiday thriller?

Oh! She could light a fire in her fireplace. She hadn't had a chance to do that in this house yet. She'd lived here almost two years, but during those two years, she'd spent all her time learning her new job and running around Portland saving people. She hadn't had the chance to just sit around in front of a fire.

Another few moments of silence. The coffee machine made a steaming noise from the kitchen behind her. She considered her cup. She should refill before she started the movie. Yeah. A refill of yummy peppermint coffee and then *Die Hard*. Perfect.

Fresh coffee, movie in the player, TV on, the first scenes of the movie—airplane landing, John McClane and his gun and stuffed bear. She shifted on the couch, looking for a more comfortable position. Her gaze went to the corner of the room next to the dogs' beds.

Christmas was only a few days away. Should she get a tree? When she'd moved here, she'd assumed that spot would be where she'd put a Christmas tree. But then, she hadn't had time for trees. Not live ones certainly. But not even time to find and put up a good artificial one. She had time now. Her bosses had promised her at least two days off. She should get a tree.

Maybe when the movie ended.

She readjusted herself on the couch. Nakatomi Plaza was about to meet Hans Gruber. She should pay attention.

Her stomach growled. Oh. Food. She needed food. An actual meal she knew wouldn't be interrupted by work. That was a treat. Almost unprecedented.

She let the movie continue rolling—she had it memorized and

could hear it from the kitchen anyway—and got herself breakfast. But since she wasn't around to cook very often, all she had was milk and cereal. Those would do. A bowl of Cheerios she didn't have to scarf down before running out to rescue some poor hapless soul. That would be nice.

The spoon scrapped the bottom of the bowl before John McClane killed his first terrorist.

She got a third cup of coffee.

Sitting forward on the couch, she tapped her feet during the first epic showdown between the hapless police and the terrorists. Had she missed "Yippee ki yay, motherfucker" or was that coming up? Well, if she'd missed it, she could watch the movie again. She had time! Glorious time.

Nothing at all to interrupt the peace.

Fred rolled onto his back, his short little legs folded and his white and brown furred belly calling for a scratch. She didn't want to wake the dogs, though. It seemed rude to disrupt their morning nap.

They'd need a walk soon, though, wouldn't they. Maybe she'd pull out the leashes and they'd go for a walk around the neighborhood. They never had time to do that. She'd bet the dogs would enjoy getting away from the house. Fred for sure would like sniffing every tree on the block.

She paused the movie mid-explosion, catching the shocked fear on John's face as a fireball raced up an elevator shaft toward him. She grinned at the screen, then said, "Guys, you want to go for a walk?"

Technically, only Buck and Fred were "guys." Pickles helped keep the balance of girls to boys in the house. But she didn't seem to object to be called "guys." Fred bounded up, a little awkwardly as he rolled back onto his stomach, and then jumped about a foot in the air. Pickles and Buck lumbered up more slowly, but Buck's tongue hung out in a happy Labrador grin and Pickles let out a deep basset woof of approval for the walk idea.

The tree-lined street was relatively empty at this time of the morning, the houses quiet, most of the driveways empty and plenty of street parking. Everyone was out at work. Or Christmas shopping. Or had left to visit relatives for the holidays. So she and the dogs didn't meet any other dogs on the entire walk.

No attacking werewolves or misbehaving goblins either.

That was a relief of course.

Back home, Cary replaced the leashes in her mudroom at the back of the house and got the dogs a little post-walk treat. It was almost Christmas after all. If you couldn't give out treats now, when could you? Fred bounced off her thigh in thanks. Buck bumped his large head against her hip, and Pickles accepted Cary's scratch behind the ear.

They passed through the kitchen on the way back to the living room and she glanced at the coffee machine. She should make another pot of coffee. She wasn't going to get interrupted by work, no running out to rescue the day today. She could afford another pot. It wouldn't go to waste this time.

She cradled more peppermint coffee as she watched the rest of the movie, her toes tapping as she watched Al Powel finally draw his gun to shoot the last terrorist. She sighed at John McClane covering his wife with his own body in that scene. So romantic. Speaking of protectors.

Huh. That *was* actually what she did all the time. Although, to be fair, she had magic she channeled—provided by her bosses and which she didn't actually control herself—that would have stopped any bullets the terrorist fired before they got to John and his wife. If she'd been there, she wouldn't have drawn a gun, since she didn't know how to fire one anyway. She'd have just jumped between John and Holly, her shields would go up, and the bullets would slam against the magic without anyone getting hurt. She was a walking, talking Kevlar vest.

But fortunately, she didn't have to worry about doing *that* today.

She carried her now empty mug back into the kitchen, humming *Let It Snow* and contemplating what to do next. She could do laundry. She always had to throw in random loads while hurrying out to save someone. She could catch up. Get ahead of things a little.

She paced to the mudroom door, turned and walked back to her refrigerator. Too early for lunch, probably. Hands in her jeans' pockets, she rocked back on her heals as she contemplated her white Frigidaire. The water-ice dispenser tray needed a cleaning.

"Christmas tree!"

She spun around and return to the living room. That spot in the corner, between the bay window and the fireplace, really would be the perfect spot for a tree. She hadn't done any decorating yet, outside of the little snowman ornament her parents had given her before leaving for New York. The snowman was surrounded by grapes and holding a bottle of wine—her dad thought that was a funny joke because she loved wine and he was a beer drinker.

But the snowman was the only remotely Christmasy thing out. She usually didn't have time to decorate. She had a couple of days free now, though. She should decorate.

"What do you think, guys?" she said to the dogs. "That lot by the Safeway still had trees a few days ago." She'd passed it after rescuing a couple of teenagers from a gremlin, but she hadn't been able to stop. She'd needed to wash off the pig poop the gremlin had thrown at them as a parting blow of non-lethal mischief. "I'm sure they'd still have trees left. I should go get one."

Fred jumped up and bounced off her thigh, before sitting on the ground, his thick tail thumping the hard wood floor as he sat up, holding his balance by swinging his front paws in a little prayer motion. His gaze kept cutting back to the kitchen.

"Fred votes for treats and a tree. What do you two think?" she asked Buck and Pickles.

Pickles didn't raise her head from her basset hound sprawl that made her look like a basset pancake, but she did thump her tail twice in approval of the plan. Buck sat up a little, looking like a sphynx, and let his tongue loll out in a happy grin.

"Great. Treats, then I'll go get us a tree and we can decorate."

She paused halfway to the kitchen, waiting for the telltale tingle along her spine that signaled the arrival of her bosses. This was just the sort of moment when they'd show up with a job for her and she'd have to cancel the decorating plans to go rescue someone.

No tingling. No shiver of impending boss-arrival.

Huh.

Well. That was good. She really wanted a tree. And to decorate. And to have a peaceful, undisturbed couple of days.

This was great. Lovely.

Just great.

2

The smell of pine trees hit Cary the minute she opened her car door and she pulled in a deep, happy breath. She loved that smell. It would be nice to have a real tree in her house, filling it with that glorious pine scent. She couldn't remember the last time she'd gotten herself a real tree. Before becoming a Protector, for Christmas she'd driven to her parents' house, where they'd retired on the coast. Her younger sister had joined them there as well before getting married. And they'd have a family Christmas around the real tree her parents always got.

She hadn't been able to do that for the last couple of years—she couldn't afford to have her bosses pop up at her parents' house to give her a job; and she'd been pretty busy with work the last two Christmases anyway. Plus, since her *younger* sister had gotten married, her mother had upped the "encouragement" for Cary to settle down. Visits with her parents were a little more fraught these days.

But she hadn't realized how much she missed the smell of fresh pine trees until she strolled into the tree lot.

There were still several dozen trees opened and a few dozen more still tied up and stacked against the temporary chainlink fence surrounding the section of parking lot given over to the Christmas trees. Between the smell and the crisp, cold air, she was really starting to feel the holiday spirit.

Her breath puffed out in little plumes of mist as she strolled around the lot, looking for something she liked. Noble fir was her preference, but at this point she realized she couldn't be picky. Anything that smelled good and was still fresh would do.

She found a pretty, full, five-foot tall Doug fir near the back of the lot. The branches were densely packed and evenly distributed. It was very close to a perfect-looking tree. She waved down an attendant and got the tree wrapped into netting so she could get it home. She'd have to strap it to the roof of her Corolla but at only five-foot, the tree was short enough for her to carry inside on her own without having to drag it.

She bought a tree stand while she was at it, since she didn't have one, and refused the fake snow flocking with a barely contained wince. Some people liked that stuff. She just wanted a nice green tree. After dropping in some extra money for the tree replanting fund, she and the cheerful older man who'd trimmed the trunk to fit in her new stand hauled the wrapped tree up onto her car roof and carefully tied it down with twine running through her windows. Given the chilly air, she was glad she didn't have far to go since she'd have to leave the windows cracked.

She wished the nice man a happy holiday and drove home with the scent of pine sap on her hands.

Once she had the tree up, the netting around it cut away, and the base filled with water, she stood back to admire her work. The tree fit perfectly in the corner of her living room.

"What do you think, guys?" The dogs were arrayed around her in a semicircle as they all stared at the new addition to their house. "You like it?"

Pickles woofed. Buck thumped his tail a few times. Fred let loose a loud yipping bark and he jumped up against her leg to affirm his enthusiasm for the tree. Or, given he kept angling toward the kitchen, maybe he was just looking for more treats.

"Later," she told him. "Decorations first."

She paused on the way to her garage, waiting for that tingling along her spine.

Nothing.

So. Her bosses were still leaving her alone. That was good. Great. The day off was going wonderfully so far.

Not a single thing to disturb the peace.

SHE ORDERED PIZZA FOR DINNER, BECAUSE HOLIDAYS AND LOVELY peaceful quiet time alone. And also because she didn't have anything else in the house to eat. The colored lights on the tree twinkled, reflecting light off the colorful bulbs and string of golden beads encircling the thick branches. Admiring her work, she settled in with her slice of pepperoni.

"We did good," she told the dogs.

Fred sat up in anticipation of a piece of pepperoni.

They'd put up a few more decorations around the living room too. Some fake pine bunting with red ribbons along the fireplace mantel. Little blinking, colored lights over the curtain rod on the bay window. A few colorful glass bulbs hanging off random bits of furniture. And the cross-stitched picture of a cabin in the snow her sister had done for her a few years ago as a present.

That reminded her, she'd better check her package of presents had arrived at her sister's house.

She stared at the decorations as she savored melty cheese. This was good. She was really enjoying the peace and quiet.

After dinner, and getting the dishes done, and putting on a load of laundry, and cleaning out the tray under her water-ice dispenser on her fridge, Cary stood in the middle of her living room with her hands on her hips, staring at the tree.

Peace and quiet.

"Should I watch another movie?" she asked the dogs. Or maybe she should start one of the pile of novels she'd pulled out. She didn't have a radio—who had time for just listening to music—but she might be able to find something on her phone she could play. Seemed like they needed some holiday music.

She listened to the quiet. "Yeah, I'll put on another movie."

The Muppets' Christmas Carol played in the background as she sent her sister a text and contemplated the tree some more.

Maybe she'd go to bed early. She could do with some more sleep. That seemed like a good idea. Nothing else going on. No emergencies looming. Just lovely quiet.

Lovely and quiet.

3

 $\mathcal{C}$ ary woke from a sound sleep with a suddenness that made her pulse pound.

What the…?

Usually that kind of jolt awake meant her bosses were here waiting for her because she was needed somewhere. She slept in pajama pants and t-shirts for this very reason, because she never knew when her bosses might show up.

She grabbed her cellphone off her bedside table as she hurried out to her living room. Three in the morning. Yeah, probably something to do with a vampire. Or maybe a shapeshifter. Although, the last time they woke her up in the middle of the night it had been a pixie with a grudge against a gnome, so you never knew.

But when she stumbled into her living room, her bosses weren't there.

She frowned. What the hell had woken her up?

She glanced at the bay window and the dog beds underneath. Fred was still sound asleep, but both Buck and Pickles were sitting at the base of the Christmas tree looking up into the branches.

"What's going on, guys?" she asked, coming closer. She nearly

45

jumped out of her skin when she heard the scritching noise from inside the tree.

Shit. Had she brought in a mouse or a squirrel or something? She hadn't spotted anything while decorating the tree, but that didn't mean something small couldn't hide in there. For all she'd been a biology student in college, was an animal lover, and had intended on being a veterinary technician before the Protector thing, she really really didn't like mice. Especially not in her house.

She wasn't too keen on the idea of a squirrel being in here either. But that was more because Fred might decide to chase it and then there'd be mayhem. And likely some broken furniture.

She eased up to the tree, her eyes narrowed. Neither Buck nor Pickles had moved when she came out. They continued to stare into the branches.

If she turned on the flashlight app on her phone, would she startle whatever was in there and chase it out? She danced on her toes, anticipating a mouse and estimating the distance it would take to leap to the couch. She really was a wimp when it came to mice.

She winced and edged close to Buck and Pickles while trying not to get too close to the tree.

A little squeaky sound from the tree made her shiver.

The fact that the squeaky sound resolved into *words* made her straighten and glare.

"What the hell?"

A head popped out from the branches, high up on the tree. A little head, topped by green-brown hair over a brown face with a long nose and eyes so green they reminded her of the lights hanging on her tree.

Her first thought was, how the hell had a brownie gotten into her tree, and why wasn't it yowling from being around all the iron in a typical human home?

All the Fae had some sort of allergy to iron, some species worse than others. Brownies were particularly susceptible to it. There was no way that little guy should have survived a ride on top of her car.

Her very next thought was, how the hell did a brownie get *into* her home?

She had a special glamour on it, provided by her bosses, that prevented anyone from finding her house if she didn't give them permission. Which meant she could still have food delivered but she never got bothered by uninvited people selling religious pamphlets.

Close on those two thoughts, though, it struck her that the little being blinking giant green eyes at her from the middle of her Christmas tree was not, in fact, a brownie. It was smaller. Its ears were pointed and long. It was dressed in bright red clothing.

And it was cursing up a storm. In English. Like, graphic, colorful curses she didn't normally hear from members of the Fae.

"Me hat, damn it," the little creature said. "Where the feck is me hat?"

"Uh," she said.

"I have to find me hat! Don't you understand? Don't you speak? Where the feck is me hat? I need me hat. It's almost too late. I have to have me hat."

She raised her hands in a gesture she hoped would placate the little guy. "Hold on. Slower, please. You've lost your hat, but… Why would it be in my Christmas tree? And what are you doing in there? And how the hell did you get in here?"

Especially when nothing should have gotten in without her permission. Couldn't just sneak inside to get past the glamour or she'd have things sneaking in here all the time.

"Been in this fecking tree all year, haven't I? Been here just waiting. But I need me hat. Who the hell are you? Why have you stolen me hat?"

"I haven't stolen anything," she said slowly. "This is my house. My name is Cary."

"You're just a mundane human. Why can you see me?"

Good question. "What are you?"

"I'm an elf, aren't I? You eejit. Now where the feck is me hat?"

"I don't know," she said, starting to get really annoyed now. "Stop talking about your damned hat for a minute and explain to me why you were in that tree for a year?"

"That's where we Christmas tree elves live, now, isn't it? Where the hell else would I be?"

Christmas tree elves? What was that? "You ever heard of this?" she asked Buck and Pickles.

Neither responded. They just continued to look at the little elf in the tree.

Fred continued to sleep. She was more than a little surprised the noise hadn't woken him up. Not because he was a great guard dog or anything, but because conversation to Fred might mean food was involved and he never wanted to miss out on food.

"How can you see me?" the elf demanded again. "Or hear me?"

"I don't know. You're in my house, and you're making a lot of noise. Why wouldn't I hear or see you?"

"Mundanes don't see us, do they? Wouldn't be right. Would ruin everything."

"Huh?"

"I need me hat," the elf shouted.

She shushed him with a hand gesture. "Look, if I help you find your hat, will you stop yelling and maybe explain what's happening?"

"Can't promise an explanation. I'll stop shouting. Witches can see us. You a witch or something?"

She got that occasionally. "Something," she said. "Now were did you leave your hat?"

"Don't know, now do I? If I remembered, I'd be able to find it."

Cary rolled her eyes. "Can I turn on the lights? That might help."

"No! No lights, you eejit." He pointed at his eyes. "You want to blind me?"

"Wow." She sighed and edged closer to the tree, moving around Buck and Pickles because they wouldn't budge.

"Call off yer beasts," the elf said. "I ain't here to hurt anyone."

"I'm glad to hear it," Cary said. "But I think I'll let them hang out until we've got you on your way." She started nudging branches this way and that. "What does your hat look like?"

The elf had ducked back into the tree again, so his voice came out a little muffled. "It's red and got a white ruff around the base, like. And it's got a little bell at the peak."

The bell should make it easier. If she shook enough branches, they were sure to hear it.

Unfortunately, most of the little glass ball ornaments she'd hung also made tinkling noises when they bounced around.

She sighed. "This would be a lot easier with light."

"No light!"

"Can I at least turn on the tree lights? They're not as bright as regular lights. They might help."

The elf poked his head back out from the branches, this time close enough to Cary she had to swallow a gasp.

"Tree lights, eh? Are they white?"

"Colored."

"Blinky? I hates blinky."

"I don't have to turn on the blinky part."

"Why the hell would you get blinky?"

"I like the twinkle."

"No blinking. But yeah, they might help, like."

"Okay." She plugged in the lights, breathing slowly in and out so she didn't let her irritation show. Too much. "How's that?"

"Good, good." The voice from inside the tree now. The little elf poked his head back out a moment later. He was higher in the branches, near the peak of the tree. "You still helping or not?"

She shook her head, but started gently moving branches around the base of the tree. "It would help if I understood what was going on," she said.

She lifted a string of the golden bead garland to see farther back in the tree. Even with the lights on, the spaces near the trunk were shadowed and dark. A red hat should be obvious in those shadows, though, right? At least one with a white ruff around it. Maybe not the red.

She moved on to the next branch. Buck and Pickles continued to remain steadfastly in place, staring up into the tree.

"Do you guys know what's happening?" she asked them. Not so much as a tail wag in response.

She glanced at the still sleeping Fred. This was really…

Well, she'd been about to think odd, but outside of her dogs being here, this sort of weirdness had actually become her normal.

"Try that branch over there," the elf snapped.

She looked up to see him pointing a little farther over on the tree. "I'll finish here first. If we're not methodical, we'll miss something."

"We don't have time for methodical," the elf snarled. "We've got to find me fecking hat."

"And we will if you'll just calm down," Cary said as calmly as she could manage. Middle of the night, getting yelled at by something called a Christmas tree elf, still a few days away from Christmas. And he's in a hurry.

Did make her extremely curious what the hurry was.

"If I can't find me hat, they'll come, don't ye see? They'll be released. And then where will we be? Fecked, that's where. We have to find that hat."

Okay, that was more than he'd given her so far. "Who…or what are 'they,' and why shouldn't they be released?"

"You want hopelessness sweeping the land, do you then? You want them to win?"

"I… No. Hopelessness?" She moved a swinging ball ornament out of her face to check deeper into the tree again. She'd gotten a really really thick and dense tree. That had seemed like a good idea at the lot.

"Hopelessness, you eejit. Hopelessness. You want to live in a land full of hope or one full of hopelessness?"

"Continuing to call me an eejit doesn't reassure me that you're a creator of hope," she said in a mild tone.

"You even know what eejit means?"

"Of course I do. It's kind of obvious."

A little head popped out of the tree right in front of her face. She gasped because it was impossible not to when an elf suddenly appeared in front of your face even though you'd just been having a conversation with him.

"Christmas tree elves don't make the hope," he said, his voice low and intense. "The hope is someone else's job. My job is to ensure the hopelessness doesn't get out."

"And you need your hat to do that?"

Green eyes too large for the little face blinked slowly at her. "Yes."

"And you're running out of time?"

Another slow blink. "Yes."

"Then why aren't you still searching?"

Another series of colorful curses—she'd have to ask Jaxer what gobshite meant to be sure, but she had a pretty good guess—accompanied the elf as he ducked back into the tree.

Cary continued her search of the lower branches, having to squish herself between the wall and the tree when she got around to the back. One little glass ball fell and she couldn't snatch it fast enough to keep it from hitting the ground. Fortunately, it landed on the tree skirt and not the wooden floor. The last thing she needed was shattered glass she couldn't see well enough to clean up right now.

She scooped up the ball, but stopped mid-motion rehanging the ornament. A sound halfway between a whine and a growl from the other side of the tree had her rushing back out from behind it, scrapping against sharp needles in the process.

"Buck, was that you?"

Pickles and Buck had both turned away from the tree and were now facing the center of the living room.

Where a white misty fog rose from the hardwood floor.

Well.

That wasn't good.

4

"*U*hm," Cary said to the Christmas tree elf still rustling around in her tree as the white fog crept across her living room floor. "Want to explain the mist?"

And how the hell it had gotten into her house?

It was thick and swirling in a breeze that wasn't there, coalescing into little spherical bundles of denser fog. Almost like something was…forming inside the mist.

She moved to stand between her dogs and the mist, ensuring the dogs and her tree were safely in her protection. Her shields went up automatically when there was a threat. So long as the dogs, and the Christmas tree elf, stayed behind her, she should be able to protect them from the white fog. Whatever it was.

She called to Fred, trying to wake him up and get him to move closer, but he didn't even roll over in his sleep. He did issue a little whiney snore that reassured her he was still okay. But having him outside her protection when…something had gotten into the house made her nerves pop.

Bad guys weren't supposed to find her house without her permission, nonetheless get *inside* her house. She could explain away the elf being here. Technically, she supposed, she'd invited him in when she brought his tree in. But the fog had most definitely not been invited.

"That's them, that's them," the elf said, his voice going higher in his panic. "I gots to find me hat."

"You search. I'll keep…them from getting to you," she said.

"How?"

"Just… Look are they bad guys, whatever they are?"

"Hopelessness is always bad," the elf snarled.

She got the feeling he'd bit his tongue on calling her an eejit again. "And you're, sort of, the good guy who stops hopelessness?"

"Yes, yes, yes."

"And if they get to you before you find your hat, that would be bad?"

"Yes!"

"Then find your damn hat," she snapped. "I can hold off bad guys to keep good guys safe."

"How?"

"It's what I do. Stop messing around and find your hat."

She didn't go into further detail. She didn't tell people what she was or what she could do. When she wasn't protecting someone, when she wasn't channeling the magic her bosses gave her, she was an ordinary human woman and could be killed as easily as the next human. She was safer the fewer people who knew what she was— because if they didn't know, they wouldn't be able to learn the loophole in her magic that could get her killed.

She heard the frantic curses and swaying of the tree behind her but kept her gaze on the coalescing fog. A faint sound rose from the depths of the mist now, a sound like moaning. She shivered.

That was a little too close to ghosts for her. She hated ghosts. They scared the shit out of her.

But she was pretty certain this, whatever it was, wasn't a ghost. Right?

"They're not ghosts?" she asked the elf.

"Course not. They were never living things to be dead now. They're…hopelessness."

"Didn't know it had a form," she muttered as the spheres of dense fog elongated into upright ovals.

"They *are* things. Just not like a living thing that died."

"Well, that's good then."

Maybe. The shapes these things were taking on looked an awful lot like skeletons. And in the region of what she assumed were faces, eyes starting winking into existence. Red eyes like a demon's.

The moans grew louder.

Next to her, Pickles let out a deep woof, and Buck growled quietly.

"Not liking this either, guys," she said.

She glanced at Fred. Still sound asleep. He was breathing, she could see his little side moving up and down, but otherwise, he wasn't moving. Guess he'd caught the squirrel and moved on to a less active dream.

She faced the approaching fog again.

Approaching.

Shit.

"Whatever they are, they're getting closer," she said.

The elf squeaked.

"They won't reach you," she assured. "I've got this part. But you maybe need to find your hate soonish."

"You think I don't know it," the elf snarled.

She didn't turn to look, but she got the impression he'd stuck his head out of the tree again because his voice was less muffled. "Stop wasting time yelling at me."

More cursing.

The fog of skeletal hopelessness got to within a foot of her before stopping. The line of her shield became visible at the edge of the fog, where it piled up and couldn't move any further. The skeletal shapes within the fog scrambled at the edges with bone-like fingers, but couldn't get past. She only ever saw her shield when something like this encountered it. She couldn't feel it, just had to trust it was there. After two years, she did trust the magic now. But it was still nice to see it working so clearly.

The red eyes inside the hopelessness skeletons blinked and

flickered. That was weird. They reminded her a little of her Christmas tree lights. Except…creepy. Without all the other pretty things strung around them, they definitely weren't charming.

The moaning grew louder.

She wanted to ask the elf how he was doing but she was afraid he'd get distracted cursing at her again. She set a hand onto Buck's big head. He stood just behind her, staying within her protection, which pleased her. Pickles did too, which was nice. She'd have preferred having Fred close—she didn't have to protect *inside* her house like this normally; it was scary having her dogs in danger—but the fog didn't seem to have any interest in him. It didn't flow his way. It didn't come within two yards of him.

In fact…

She frowned. Huh. It almost looked like the fog was…avoiding Fred. There was a big bubble of clear air all around him. None of the skeleton things even reached toward him or looked in his direction. They were all focused on her and the tree behind her. It was almost like they didn't know he was there.

Well, that was…good?

Definitely a relief. But Fred was about as ordinary a dog as you could get. And she couldn't protect him from this distance, not in a separate bubble shield like that. This wasn't anything to do with her magic. So why was the hopelessness avoiding him?

Weird.

She let out a low breath and finally said to the elf, "Any luck?"

"Ah, wait, wait now…"

She thought he was going to start cussing again, but suddenly a happy—and piercing—shout came from the tree.

"I found it! I found the bleeding thing."

His whoops made her smile.

"Great news. Now get out here and get rid of all this hopelessness in my house. I can't have this stuff here."

She couldn't afford to lose hope. Her entire job was built on hope. Hope that one person could stop bad guys from hurting good guys, at least some of the time. Hope that the magic she channeled would work when she needed it to. Hope that nothing would be strong enough to get through that magic. Hope that she would get between the bad guys and the good guys in time.

She needed hope to survive her job. She couldn't afford to let hopelessness take over.

There was a metaphor in there somewhere, she was sure.

The elf leapt from the tree and landed next to Pickles, just behind and to the right of Cary. Pickles glanced at him—he was small enough for her to eat—then focused on the skeleton fog again.

The moaning from the skeletons was even louder now, loud enough to make Cary wince.

"Now would be good to do…whatever you need to do," she told the elf.

"Don't hurry an artist," he snapped.

She glared down at him. Now that he wasn't hiding in the tree and she could see him better, she realized he looked a little like a tree. Although his outfit was red, not green like the pine branches, his entire body was as brown as the tree trunk, and patterned almost like bark where it peaked out of his red jacket and pants. The outfit had a pine needle pattern on it as well. If he'd been wearing green, he would have looked just like the tree.

He stared down the skeletons, all of whom had changed focus to the elf. They clustered toward him, their moans so loud Cary had no idea how Fred was sleeping through all this. Thanks to her magic the skeletons didn't get close to the elf, but they scrabbled against her shield with their bony fingers trying to reach him.

He held out his hat, holding it between the fog and himself like he was holding up a trophy. It was just as he'd described it. Red and pointed with a white fur trim circling the base and a little bell at the peak. Just like a Santa Claus hat actually. He said something in a language Cary didn't know—there were a lot of vowels involved though—and slowly…

Put the hat onto his head.

5

The moans inside the skeleton fog grew louder, turning into cries of denial, almost like pain. The skeletons started to move backward, toward the darker sections of Cary's living room.

The elf moved out from behind her, walking toward the fog.

She opened her mouth to stop him, but paused when she realized he was glowing now. With the hat in place, he was alight with an inner glow that turned his bark-like skin into a sparkling glory. And his outfit was as bright as a tiny sun. She squinted as she looked at him, no longer able to see his face through all that light.

Shadows danced around her living room, retreating in the face of the Christmas tree elf's sparkling, glowing glory.

The hopelessness fog churned in a furious motion, the skeleton shapes vanishing as it spun itself up like a tornado, though the red pinpoints of their eyes continued to blink in and out inside the fog. The cries were tortured now, denial and pain.

She shivered and buried her fingers deeper into Buck's thick blond fur.

The elf's light washed over the fog as he neared it, setting it aglow.

To her amazement, all the swirling and movement didn't knock anything in her living room over. No books blown off the table. No crashing furniture. All the chaos seemed to wash over her home without touching or affecting the physical world around it.

The fog glowed brighter. The elf chanted something she could barely hear now over the noise from the fog. Cary's heartbeat hammered for reasons she couldn't fully explain.

The glowing mist twirled into a tight, bright line, sparks and lights dancing along the interior like little winking stars. The red had vanished. The rope of fog folded in on itself, tighter and tighter, smaller and smaller, down to a tiny glowing sphere.

The elf snatched the tiny white ball out of the air, and popped it onto the point of his hat where the bell was.

A flash of explosive light.

Cary raised her hand to her eyes to block the glare, blinking as it faded, spots dancing in her vision.

When the spots cleared, she stared at the elf in awe. He was a little larger than he'd been, though still not big. His hat now had a little white fur ball on its top point. And his entire outfit, hat and all, had turned green.

He looked exactly like a pine tree now. A pine tree topped with a little snow.

Wow.

"Well that was impressive." Whatever he'd done. "What did you do?"

"Took care of the hopelessness, didn't it?" he said, his tone not even a little less snarly.

She was sort of glad for that. She'd have freaked out if he'd suddenly started being nice to her. "What happens now?"

"Now, I takes this stuff out of this realm so the hope spreader elves can get to work. Busy time of year, you know. Can't waste time talking to the likes of ye."

She raised her brows at the little guy. He shrugged and rolled his eyes.

"Thanks," he said. "For whatever you did with your shield. Gave me time to find me hat." His tone was gruff and he didn't meet her gaze as he spoke. "Never had help from a mortal before. You aren't a witch, huh?"

"No."

"Huh."

"Can I ask you one more question before you go?"

"Make it quick." He folded his arms over his chest, all but tapping his foot in his impatience.

"Why did the fog avoid Fred?" She nodded to her still sleeping dog. His little feet were moving again. Apparently, he was back to chasing the squirrel.

The elf stared at Fred for a long moment. "Ah. That one. He's nothing but hope. Course the hopelessness would avoid him. Like an antidote to the stuff, he is. They'd tried to touch him, they'd have shriveled to dust."

"Oh." That was so sweet. She smiled at her Fred. He really was a bundle of hope, but…wow.

"Don't start crying on me, now, woman," the elf said. "I've no time for it."

"Get out of here and take that hopelessness with you," she said, but she smiled when she did.

"What's yer name again?"

"Cary. You?"

"Herald."

"Herald?"

"Yeah, what of it?"

"Nothing. It's a good name." She smiled. "Happy holidays, Herald."

"You too," he said, snarling.

But she could tell his heart wasn't in it.

He leapt back into the tree, she heard a scrambling noise, some of the bulbs shook, and then he appeared at the point of her tree next to the ribbons she'd used as a tree topper.

He tipped his hat to her, spun in a circle, and disappeared in a beautiful flash of bright white light.

"Huh." She looked down at Buck and Pickles. They were also staring up at the tree, but Pickles had flopped onto her stomach and was looking up through the folds on her face. Buck's tail thumped against the floor twice and he looked up at her with his tongue hanging out in his doggy smile.

Fred remained resolutely asleep.

"Well, that was…interesting," she said. "You think we're good to go back to sleep now?"

Pickles let out a soft woof.

Fred, hearing the woof, rolled to his feet and scurried over, sitting up in front of her, his paws waving in the air in the little prayer hands as he worked to hold his balance.

"You missed all the excitement, Fred." Her dog full of hope. And right now, he seemed to be hoping for a treat. "All right. We've just had a little adventure. I think we've earned a late night treat."

Fred barked and raced ahead of her, bouncing in the air as he neared the kitchen door.

Cary glanced back at the tree. "Think I'll leave the lights on tonight. They're pretty." She looked at the dogs. "You guys won't mind, will you?"

Fred charged back and bounced off her leg before racing into the kitchen.

"Guess that's a no."

She followed the dogs, shaking her head. It had been, well actually, a pretty normal night for her. The full day of uneventful quiet…

Now that had been weird.

CARY'S GALENTINE'S DAY

Who needs Valentine's Day when you have Trouble…

For Cary Redmond, Portland's resident magical Protector, a simple night out with her friends to celebrate an alternative to Valentine's Day should involve good food, too much wine, and plenty of girl talk. What it actually involves is…a lot more dangerous.

But saving the innocent is what Cary does. Even on pretend national holidays.

And when called to save someone from the manipulative dangers of a wizard, Cary races to the rescue. Her friends at her back. Her wine buzz left behind.

Because no one messes with love on Cary's watch.

1

Cary smoothed down her skirt and fluffed her hair, studying her makeup in the long mirror hanging on the back of her bedroom closet door. Not bad. Not bad. The black skirt had a little flip around her knees which made her look nice-curvy instead of too hippy. The black silk shirt was made by her best friend Marianne—a weaver with actual magical skills with needle and thread—so it fit perfectly without gaping over her chest and straining the shirt buttons. She'd managed makeup, even if it was light, and left her hair down, which she rarely did.

Overall… Yeah, she felt cute.

Perfect for a night out with the girls in which they thumbed their noses at Valentine's Day.

Not that she was a big time Valentine's Day hater. That was Lucy. Lucy detested the holiday with a white hot rage that was a little terrifying from the barely five foot tall red-headed martial arts expert. To sooth her annual grumpiness, Marianne—the only one of them actually in a relationship at the moment—suggested they celebrate Galentine's Day instead. A night out, just the four friends. And they'd all agreed enthusiastically.

Cary checked the time on her cellphone, then tucked the phone and

65

her keys into the pocket of her handy leather jacket. The jacket didn't go with her outfit, but she didn't really care. It was also Marianne-made, this one with magic pockets that kept her keys, wallet, and cellphone from falling out. So if Cary's job called and she had to go jumping between good guys and bad guys to keep the good guys safe, she was all set.

With luck her job wouldn't call tonight. Being the only magical Protector in Portland did have its drawbacks, not least of which was the fact that she rarely got more than a few days without having to go rescue someone from some sort of danger. After more than four years of doing this job, she was sort of used to the spontaneousness of it now. And at least she got paid for it. Still, she really hoped tonight would be one of those nights when she could just enjoy dinner and drinks with her friends without the having to stop all hell from breaking loose.

Again.

She gave her reflection one last glance. "Think it'll do guys?" she asked her three dogs.

Her golden Labrador, Buck, who was actually a demon dog but they rarely talked about that, gave a soft snort from his perch by her bedroom door and settled his head on his paws. She took that as a yes.

Fred, the mundane collie-terrier cross in her little pack, bounced toward her in his enthusiasm. Which was nice except his fur was white and light brown and she was wearing all black. "Maybe less jumping more barking," she suggested as she gently turned him away from his attempt to climb her leg.

"What about you, Pickles?" Pickles was her basset hound, really a foo lion in retirement, and the only girl in the small pack of animals. Even the stray cat Stinky who Cary occasionally fed was very definitively boy. So Pickles and Cary had to stick together.

Pickles gave an enthusiastic woof before sprawling back onto the bedroom floor, her body nearly flat, her jowls spreading out around her snout. Cary called that her basset pancake flounce. But the woof had definitely conveyed approval.

"Thanks, guys. I appreciate the support."

And at least this wasn't a date where she had to be actually nervous and stuff. In fact, she'd been pretty lean on dates since becoming a Protector. There had been that one man a few months ago. But having to run out in the middle of dinner on their fourth date to protect another man from a ticked off lion shifter who'd caught the man cheating hadn't endeared her to the man she was supposed to be on a date with.

To be fair, the lion shifter had had a point. Cary would have been ticked off at the cheater, too. That didn't justify trying to rip his head, quite literally, off. Still, Cary had abandoned her date to help the lion shifter work through her breakup issues in a less violent manner— which involved wine, ice cream, and a lot of talking—and forgotten to call her date and let him know she wasn't coming back to the restaurant. That had been the end of *that* budding relationship.

Frankly, while she blamed her job for her abysmal dating life, she was starting to wonder if she just wasn't very good at relationships.

"But tonight is not the night to worry about it," she told her little dog pack. "Tonight, the girls and I eat, drink, and are merry. And try to keep Lucy from going on an anti-Valentine's Day rant."

She kissed doggie heads then left to meet her friends at the Italian restaurant they'd been saving for a special occasion, hopeful for a fun, uneventful evening.

"It's a scam, a conspiracy of the retailers to get our money," Lucy declared in her high-pitched, little girl's voice while sipping her fifth glass of Merlot.

The wine sloshed dangerously close to the rim of her glass as she shoved it forward to emphasize her point, but she managed to keep it from spilling. Which impressed the hell out of Cary since she'd already managed to spill a tiny bit of wine and some of her water, and she was only two glasses in. Lucy had gotten a head start on the rest of them.

"They make us think we're damaged if we're not in *love* or in a relationship," Lucy continued. She had her curly red hair up in a bun that had already loosened and listed to one side. Her pale, freckled skin was flushed from all the wine, but she still managed to look button-cute in her lavender dress that clung to her petite curves. "It's a crock. I'm fine just as I am."

"Yeah you are," Angie said, raising her glass to Lucy. "You're perfect."

Angie, their resident witch and psychic, was a six-foot tall, pale-skinned brunette who resembled a relaxed supermodel in her stylish black trousers and purple turtleneck sweater but didn't seem to notice. Her life was her psychic reading business, her family back in New Mexico, and her friends. As far as Cary could tell, Angie didn't date much either. She'd claimed she was too busy for dating when Cary had thought once to ask. Angie wasn't asexual or aromantic. She'd have told them all that years ago if she was. She just had things to do and those things didn't involve dating, apparently.

Lucy's love life, on the other hand, had been a fraught situation ever since Cary had known her. Lucy had a habit of falling for the worst men, getting her heart broken, and then spending a few weeks taking out her heartbreak on the students of her martial arts dojo. They always came out of those phases at a higher skill level than they went in, but Cary couldn't imagine the classes were a lot of fun during those weeks.

"And that asshole Derrick didn't deserve you," Marianne said, giving Lucy a little salute with her own wine.

Marianne had glammed up for their night out, too, wearing one of her custom-made dresses. This one a wrap dress that showed off her magnificent figure in an electric light blue color that reminded Cary of the color of some magic spells and looked particularly good against Marianne's dark brown skin. She always had great lipstick colors, and tonight was no exception with a bold red that worked particularly well for the holiday. She was spending Valentine's Day with her long time girlfriend, Gina, the next night. But she never hesitated to take her single friends up on a night out.

The waiter arrived with their starters, bruschetta and small plates of pasta, which made Cary's stomach growl. She'd been hungry before coming out, and she loved Italian food. Based on the bread and wine alone, this place already lived up to its reputation—little slow for the food to arrive, worth it once it did.

Garlic and olive oil and basil permeated the air around the table as they continued trying to talk Lucy down from her Valentine's Day rant. Really sort of pointless. Lucy would continue until she was done, get tired of the topic, and move on in her own time. But still they tried.

And by the time the main course arrived—Cary got a mozzarella-stuffed chicken parmesan dish that oozed with enough cheese to make her happy for a week—Lucy had segued into something less adamantly anti-Valentine's Day, though still on the topic of romance as she told them a story about two of her students getting engaged.

The wine flowed, the food was delicious, and Cary was prepared to call Galentine's Day a rousing success.

Right up until she got that warning tingle along her spine that meant someone needed her particular brand of help.

2

Cary scanned the restaurant. The trouble didn't seem to be coming from inside. In fact, she was feeling the overwhelming urge to move, to go…somewhere. She stood, plucking her jacket from the back of her chair and stuffing her arms into it as she continued scanning the restaurant.

"What's up?" Angie said, rising to her feet.

"Problem. Somewhere. Gotta go."

"We're going with you," Lucy said, rising, and then abruptly dropping back into her chair. "Shit. I'm drunk."

"Yeah you are," Marianne said.

"It's cute when you say shit, though," Cary said.

"You owe me a drink for that crack," Lucy said.

"Deal. Later. I… Yup, need to go."

"We got the bill," Marianne said. "If lovely Lucy can stand, we'll follow you."

"Thanks," Cary said.

Without further comment, Angie followed Cary outside.

Cary knew her friends would take care of things at the restaurant, and all of them could take care of themselves. She did worry when they followed her into a Protector situation, though. She could keep them safe when they were there, which was good. And all three of them had some sort of offensive skill to defend themselves against bad guys—which, ironically, Cary did not. Her Protector magic was purely defensive. She could stand between good guys and bad guys forever. But she couldn't actually attack or fight a bad guy, despite Lucy's best efforts to teach her self-defense.

Still, she always worried when they were in the middle of one of her jobs.

"Which way?" Angie asked once they stood on the sidewalk outside the restaurant.

They were in an area of downtown surrounded by little boutique stores and restaurants, not too far from one of the best donut places in the city. They'd intended to treat themselves to a late-night donut after dinner. Cary was gonna be pissed if her job prevented that treat on a national holiday.

Or the day before the holiday?

Whatever. She'd be ticked off if she didn't get a donut.

She followed her instincts wordlessly and Angie followed her, staying just behind her so Cary's Protector magic would already be working if danger stepped out in front of them. Her magic *only* worked when she was protecting someone, or jumping in between good guys and bad guys. And if she had to jump in between something moving fast, like a bullet, or a wizard bolt, she sometimes got hurt. Nothing fatal. But the bruises and weird bone cracks were always hard to explain to ER staff.

She turned down a narrow side street, blocked off to be a pedestrian walkway so no cars could drive here, and narrow enough it could have been an alley. Most of the stores were closed this time of night, the street lights giving everything a soft golden glow.

That didn't hide the shadows in a doorway two stores up.

From a distance, it just looked like two people talking, a tall man standing inside the doorway, a smaller woman leaning into him. But when the woman raised her hand, and a swirling ball of blue light formed on the center of her palm, Cary's instincts kicked in hard.

She raced forward—despite her heels, though she'd feel that later

—and dove between the man and woman seconds before the wizard bolt hit the man. Instead, it thumped into Cary's shield, a little of the electrical zing shivering across her nerves. She shook her shoulders hard.

Crappy way to have her wine buzz shocked out of her.

She raised her palms, face out when the woman snarled at her and raised her hand again, another wizard bolt forming on her palm.

"Get out of the way," the woman hissed. "He's mine. I found him first."

"Uh, that's…" Cary shook her head. "I'm not sure what's happening, but no hitting people with wizard bolts on my watch."

The woman smirked. "Not a wizard bolt. And this isn't your business."

"Looked like you were about to kill…" She looked over her shoulder. To the man, she said, "Hi. I'm Cary. You got a name?"

"Alan." He blinked at her, blinked at his surroundings. "What's happening?"

Almost like he was coming out of a daze. That was…probably not good.

Alan was a couple inches taller than Cary, closer to Angie's six-foot height—though, since Angie was no longer behind her and she couldn't see Angie anywhere, which was *extremely worrying,* she couldn't make the actual comparison. He was a handsome young man, in that way that required looking twice to really see it, but once you looked at him closer you got the appeal. His black hair was cut in a shortish but fluffy style that suited him, had pale skin and dark brown eyes, was on the thin side but broad-shouldered, and had a lean, angular face that held a lot of interest. He was dressed in nice, dark blue trousers and a thick wool coat that looked warm enough for the cold February night, but the breeze blowing through his hair made Cary shiver for some reason even though her leather jacket was more than warm enough too.

Alan also looked very confused. "Where am I?" he asked. "What's going on?"

Yeah, that wasn't good. "Don't worry. I've got you now. You're safe."

"Get out of my way," the woman snapped at Cary, drawing her attention again. "He's mine."

"You know this woman, Alan?" Cary asked, her gaze steady on the woman, who hadn't released or dropped the ball of swirling blue energy on her palm that she claimed wasn't a wizard bolt.

She was shorter than Cary, with very blond hair, dark blue eyes, and what Cary's mother would call a "patrician" nose. She wasn't a bad looking woman. She wasn't stunning or anything, but she was nice enough looking and had done a good job with her hair and makeup to give herself a glamourous appearance, even if her features were a little tight and maybe too narrow. She was wearing a pretty black dress that had sparkles all over it under an open, long black trench coat, and high, spiked heels that gave Cary vertigo just looking at them.

They also reminded her she'd probably turned her ankle running to get here in her own significantly lower heels.

"I've never seen her before," Alan said about the woman. "Who are you?"

Cary couldn't tell if he was asking her that question or the woman.

"What's that ball of blue on your hand? Is that one of those party trick things?"

Okay, talking to the woman.

"Not a party trick, I'm afraid," Cary said about the woman's wizard bolt… Or whatever it was. She'd said it wasn't a wizard bolt, but she'd known what a wizard bolt was, so…probably dealing with a wizard.

Magic. Fun.

That was more Angie's domain, and the fact that Angie had disappeared somewhere was starting to really worry Cary. She usually stuck close to Cary in these situations because it helped keep everyone safe if Cary was protecting her.

Angie's witch magic took time—she cast spells and getting a spell to work right, without backfiring on the witch casting it, took words and hand gestures all done in precisely the right way. Angie couldn't call energy bolts the way a wizard could. But she was a super powerful witch who'd trained for a long time. She had no trouble in most magical fights, at least not that Cary had ever witnessed.

So the fact that Angie wasn't right behind her, murmuring some sort of spell to take care of the wizard was extremely unusual and not a little scary.

Cary tried to focus on the situation at hand. Though, now that she was between the woman and the man, the man was safe and they had all the time in the world. She could wait out whatever the woman tried until the woman got bored and went away.

But she was curious enough to want to know what the wizard had been trying to do. And thinking about that helped her keep her mind off what might be going on with Angie.

"Want to explain all this?" she asked the woman. "What the hell did Alan ever do to you?"

"If I tell you he cheated on me, will you move aside?" the woman asked, sounding curious, but not particularly angry.

"I wouldn't get out of the way, but I might have had some sympathy for you. Except we've already established Alan doesn't know you."

"I don't," Alan said, starting to sound a little frantic. "I really don't."

The woman shrugged. "Just thought I'd ask."

"So what *is* all this about?" Cary said at the same time Alan said, "Why me?"

"You," the woman said, nodding at Alan, "because I need a range of men and you fit some of the descriptions. And tomorrow is Valentine's Day."

She said all that so matter-of-factly, Cary blinked a few times. "Huh?"

"It's not that complicated," the woman said. "But I don't have time to discuss it. So you'll just need to step aside so I can finish. I have enough women already. I could use some more nonbinary people if you know anyone? That's the one place I'm short."

Again, "Huh?"

The woman waved her free hand. The blue ball that wasn't a

wizard bolt still sat in her palm like a little swirling ball of St. Elmo's Fire. "Never mind. I'll get it taken care of before tomorrow. Move. I don't have time for this delay."

"Uh." Cary frowned. "I'm gonna say, no. No, I think I'll stay right here."

The woman sighed. "Suit yourself, but I already have enough of your type. I'll figure something out."

She raised the ball of whatever it was on her palm and tossed it at Cary and Alan.

3

$\mathcal{C}$ary watched the wizard's magic ball of power slam into her shield and scattered over it like water against glass, breaking apart into waves of sparkling energy. It was pretty enough, but she was still too distracted trying to figure out what the wizard intended to pay much attention.

She brought herself back to the situation when Alan grabbed her arm and gasped, and the wizard snarled a curse.

The narrow street remained blissfully quiet, with no other innocent people tromping in to complicate Cary's life. That was good at least. But the fact that Angie was still nowhere to be seen continued to bother her.

"What was that?" Alan asked at the same time as the wizard hissed, "What have you done?"

And then simultaneously, they both said, "How did you do that?" Though the woman's version of the question was said with a lot of anger, while Alan's question was full of quiet awe.

Cary waved her hand in the air and gave her usual flippant response. "Just a talent I have. No big deal."

She never told people what she was, because when she wasn't protecting someone, her powers didn't work and she was an ordinary, vulnerable human. The fewer people who knew that she was a Protector, the better. At least for her chances of survival.

"I would still like to know what you're trying to do," she said to get back on topic. She'd also like to know where Angie had gone. And for that matter, where Marianne and Lucy were. She didn't want them walking into this unprepared and getting hurt.

"I don't have time for this," the woman snapped. "Move. Now. I have…more to get to tonight."

"No. And I can stand here all night. Literally. Right here. In your way. Keeping you from hurting Alan. So you can either walk away—" and Cary wasn't so sure that was a great option since whatever the wizard was up to, she seemed inclined to keep doing it even if she didn't do whatever it was she was trying to do to Alan, "—or you can explain and we can work all this out. Or, I suppose you can keep wasting time throwing that non-wizard bolt magic at us. But it'll be a waste of time and magic, so maybe…not? Not would be good."

A blast of white hot energy shot from the woman's hand, slamming hard into Cary's shield. The move so abrupt and sudden both Cary and Alan gasped this time.

"Shit," Alan muttered. "What was that?"

"*That,*" Cary said with a nod, "was an energy bolt. A little different to a wizard bolt. Energy bolts are mostly just pure electrical energy designed to sizzle the target, sometimes incinerate them, depending."

Alan cursed under his breath.

"Yeah, not pleasant. Wizard bolts are made of actual magic, not just electrical energy, and can do a range of things, depending on the wizard. Sometimes they just kill, cause getting hit by raw magic will do that to the unprepared. Sometimes they incapacitate. Sometimes they knock a person out. It depends really. There are…levels of wizard bolts. I'm not an expert since I'm not a wizard and didn't train as one, so I'm not entirely sure how it all works. Only what I've read in books."

"What books do you read?" Alan asked, sounding aghast.

"Oh, lots of different stuff, really. Still a *lot* I don't know, though." Much to her bosses' dismay.

But hell, there was a lot of magical stuff for her to learn and every time she thought she might be making progress, something came up and she had a whole new area to study. The sheer volume of supernatural and preternatural information out there was pretty overwhelming, and she'd only been studying it all for four years now. It could take a practitioner of any given subject decades to learn most of the fundamentals. Nonetheless trying to learn everything about everything.

Try telling her bosses that, though.

She blinked back to her current situation when the wizard snarled at her again. Lot of snarling going on.

"How do you know all this if you're not a wizard?" the woman said, glaring at Cary like she could put a hole in her with a look.

Cary was a little worried if she hadn't been protecting someone the woman could have done just that.

"Like I said, I read." Cary shrugged. "Anyway, wizard bolts and trying to kill me with an energy bolt aside, what was that thing you were trying to do to Alan here? I'm still super curious."

"You're not a paying client. Why the fuck would I tell you anything?"

"Paying client? Interesting. What do they pay for?"

"Fuck you." Another energy bolt hit Cary's shield.

She was more prepared for the suddenness of it this time. Alan still jumped and his grip on Cary's arm tightened. She couldn't blame him. The lights and glare of scattering energy were pretty terrifying when they came right at you.

"Wasting energy," Cary said, absently. She hunted the narrow street, looking into nearby doorways and trying—unsuccessfully of course—to see in the shadows at the corner of the street.

Still no sign of Angie, Marianne, or Lucy. She wasn't sure whether to be glad or not. Glad they weren't in danger, sure. But still a little worried they'd walk into danger and she wouldn't be able to protect them. And also worried about what had happened to them. It wasn't like Angie to run away from a threat, especially a magical one, and since she'd followed Cary from the restaurant specifically to help her, Angie's absence was just strange.

Another few flashes of light as more wizard magic—a wizard bolt with its angry blue sizzle, a few more energy bolts, and one red blast of power Cary didn't recognize as something wizards usually did—slammed into her shield in rapid succession.

She'd have to ask Angie about that red ball of magic. That looked more like a fire ball and that was something demons did and certain witches—Angie had a spell that created a little ball of fire—but wizard magic was different to witch magic, and demon magic for that matter, so fire balls weren't typically in a wizard's repertoire.

She considered just asking the wizard outright what the red ball had been, but the woman seemed too stressed and angry to answer, so she saved that question.

She did ask, "Are you done yet?" When the powerful magic stopped slamming her shield. "That's not getting through. And whatever you'd intended for Alan isn't happening on my watch."

"Who the fuck are you?" the woman said, panting a little.

Wow, she must have really been working her powers. "Just a concerned citizen," Cary used her standard answer, "and Alan here is my current concern."

"How are you doing this?" Alan murmured close to her ear. "And *what* is happening? Is she…is she… What is all that she's…doing?"

"Sorry, I should have explained." She half turned to look at Alan, keeping the wizard in her peripheral vision, even though that wasn't strictly necessary. Now that she was standing here, she really could do this all night and keep Alan safe. No need to keep staring down the threat. Still, she liked to keep the bad guys in sight so she knew what they were getting up to.

"This woman is a wizard," Cary said. "And she's been throwing magic at us. Different spells. I'm not sure what the red ball was, but the other stuff was wizard and energy bolts. Pretty powerful. I think. Hard to tell since they're not getting through, but they look pretty powerful, right?"

"Uh huh," Alan said, sounding dazed.

"I know, it's a lot to take in. As you may have guessed, I have no idea what she was trying to do originally. You have any ideas? Maybe she said something?"

"I don't know her. I have no idea what she wants." He frowned and glanced at the ground.

Another energy bolt scattered harmlessly across Cary's shield and the wizard cursed. "Shut up."

"What's the last thing you remember?" Cary asked Alan, ignoring the wizard.

"I was coming out of work. I work at a bank. Teller."

"Nice job," Cary said, encouragingly because Alan looked like he needed a boost. The confusion creasing his brow and eyes gave him a sort of sad, lost look that made her heart hurt.

Typically, Cary didn't argue about protecting woman, or kids, or older people, or animals, or really most anyone in danger. This was her job, and jumping in to save kids or women or old people or animals was an easy ask. But there was a part of her that thought grown ass men should be able to take care of themselves, and when her bosses sent her out to protect a grown ass man, she could occasionally get a little resentful and irritated.

Okay, maybe more than occasionally. And she got irritated with her bosses on a regular basis, so that wasn't anything new. But being sent to rescue grown ass men got her *more* irritated. It was a prejudice she was well aware of and working on, but still hadn't managed to squash.

She also recognized that the prejudice was an outright falsehood in a lot of situations. Like this particular one. When the grown ass man was an ordinary human man, and the bad guy wielded magic or was a shifter or a vampire or the like, the ordinary human grown ass man really did need her help. He couldn't take care of himself. Which was why, despite her prejudice, she didn't hesitate to dive in and save grown ass men.

And in cases like this, when the man looked genuinely confused and lost and scared, well… Her prejudice died in the face of her stupid empathy.

"Keep going," she said with a little wave, keeping her voice level and calm. "What happened after you left work? Were you going right home? Stopping somewhere?"

His frown deepened. "I was planning to stop at the grocery store on the way home. My sister's having a bad time, and I thought I'd make her dinner."

"Aw, that's so nice of you." Cary didn't cook much if she could avoid it, just basics like pasta and eggs and stuff, so having someone cook for her always sounded like the most caring act of kindness.

Alan smiled faintly, a wobbly smile but still a smile. It didn't last long before he was frowning again, though. "I don't think I made it to the grocery store." He looked around as if looking for evidence one way or the other. "I don't really remember what happened after I left work. It's a blank." Panic crept into his voice. "I…I can't remember. I can't… It's not there. Just blank. What the hell happened? What's going on?"

Cary raised her hands, palms facing him, placating and trying to calm. "It's okay. You're safe now. We'll figure this out."

"How am I safe? How are you… What are you doing?"

"Just lending a helping hand. It's what I do. Let's get back to you. What time did you leave work?"

"Five thirty. When the bank closed."

It was after nine thirty now. So he'd lost four hours. No wonder he was panicked.

"Do you have a car? Are we near your bank?" she asked.

He looked around, jumping when another energy bolt hit her shield. She ignored the wizard's cursing and waited patiently for Alan to answer.

"My branch is in Hawthorne…not downtown." He scowled at the surroundings because at the moment they were definitely downtown and nowhere near Hawthorne in the south east of the city. "And I have a car. I don't see it anywhere."

To be fair, they weren't on a street where there could be street parking. But still, if his car was around here somewhere, it wasn't close by. So he likely hadn't driven here. Or if he did, it wasn't under his own influence. He hadn't intended on being in this area tonight.

She turned back to face the wizard who had her hands on her knees and was wheezing. "Wow, you're going to hurt something if you don't stop soon," Cary said. "Anyway, did you ambush Alan at work or somewhere else? And did you drive his car? Or put him in a car? And why all the way over here?"

She glanced around again. What was nearby that might require the wizard to bring Alan here?

There was a shop selling gourmet chocolate—she'd have to visit that place when it was open—and a couple of clothing and pop culture stores. There was a small, hole-in-the-wall computer repair place tucked between a vintage poster store and a coffee shop—that last almost as tempting as the chocolate for Cary—and a small tattoo parlor just behind the wizard. Most of the stores were closed this time of night, even the coffee shop unfortunately.

But along the same side of the street as she stood, a small neon sign hung out over the street, glowing pink. The sign was shaped like a heart with an arrow through it, and the words Cupid Matches written in fancy script filled in the heart's center.

Cupid Matches.

Wizard claimed to need people of certain types.

Tomorrow was Valentine's Day.

Oh boy.

4

$\mathcal{C}$ary sighed and faced the wizard just as she threw another energy bolt which scattered harmlessly across Cary's shield. Cary tisked at her. "You're magicking people to match with your clients, aren't you?"

That had to be it. There was no other reason to bring Alan all the way here when the wizard had obviously approached him somewhere near his work. If Alan couldn't remember past leaving work, and had no reason to have come downtown on his own, chances were good he didn't come here under his own influence.

He was here because the wizard brought him here. And the wizard wouldn't have brought him here for no reason.

"Tell me I'm wrong," she said to the woman.

She sort of hoped she was wrong. Because this was epic levels of sickening if she wasn't. The consent issues alone made her brain hurt and her stomach roll. What happened when the clients met these bespelled matches? What happened with the bespelled people? How far did this "match" go before the bespelled people came back to themselves?

And what the hell was a wizard doing involved in this kind of thing?

Frankly, even though one of her best friends was a witch, this was the sort of nasty turn of magic Cary expected from witches more than wizards. Wizards tended toward the big power grabs. Witches toward manipulation. That was, at a base level, closer to how their individual types of magics worked. So discovering a wizard doing this kind of manipulation game seemed... Well, odd.

The woman glared at Cary, her face pinched with frustration, her jaw so tight, she looked like she might crack her teeth. "This is none of your business, witch. Get out of my fucking way. I have a job to do."

"No. And not a witch. And again, no. Alan here didn't sign up for your little matchmaking scheme." At least she assumed he hadn't, but... "Did you sign up for a matchmaking scheme for Valentine's Day?" she asked him. "Or maybe a dating site or something?"

"No," he said. "I just got out of a relationship before Christmas and haven't been up to dating again yet."

"I'm sorry about your relationship," Cary said.

He waved her sympathies away. "It was mutual. We're still in touch. I'm just not ready to start anything new."

"Fair enough. I get that."

"Would you two shut up," the wizard snapped. "This isn't about him."

"I beg to differ," Cary said. "You were manipulating him with magic. I'm going to assume you brought him here for some sort of nefarious matchmaking thing given the clues you've dropped already. And that's not okay when he didn't sign up for it. In fact, it's pretty skeevy. So this has everything to do with him, and I'm not letting you hurt him."

"He wouldn't be hurt. A date isn't going to hurt him. One night of inane small talk."

"If that were the case, you wouldn't need magic. You could pay people."

"I'm not running an escort agency," the woman bit out as if offended.

Which struck Cary as hypocritical given she was using magic on the unwilling—not even a little honest—and an escort agency with proper pay and consent was straightforward and fully honest as far as businesses went. In fact, Cary took offense at the wizard's offense. Looking down on hard working escorts and their clients was rude.

"Well, you're obviously crap at matchmaking, or you wouldn't need to use magic against unwilling people," Cary said. "I'd recommend a different line of work." Another energy bolt hit Cary's shield. She shook her head as the flash of light cleared. "Stop that. You're wasting your time."

"What…what are we supposed to do now?" Alan asked quietly behind her.

"She'll get bored eventually and leave. Or the lightshow will attract attention and she'll leave."

"Or I'll kill you and get what I'm here for," the wizard said.

"Sure sure. Except you won't."

"You think I can't break down your shield, witch?"

"Told you, not a witch. And yes, I think I'm safe from your magic in this moment. So is Alan. No tricking unwilling people into this weird matchmaking thing." Cary frowned. "By the way, and just out of curiosity, what do you get out of all this? I can't imagine the money is good enough to make all this magic use and risk worth your while."

"You'd be wrong. You have no idea what people are willing to do to have a date for Valentine's Day."

Cary ignored the wizard's smirk. "That's sad." She turned a little to look at Alan. "Don't you think that's sad? I mean, the pressure of society telling people they *have* to have a date for Valentine's Day or else they're miserable and loveless? That's just so wrong."

"Yeah, it's a tough time of year," Alan said, though he was mostly staring through narrowed eyes at the wizard.

"I have a friend who hates this holiday with a passion," Cary said. "Even when she's dating someone, she hates this holiday."

"I can understand that," Alan said. "Not a fan myself. Getting to be less of a fan as the night progresses."

Cary snorted. "Yeah."

"Would you two shut up," the wizard said, sounding almost as baffled as she was annoyed.

"What else are we going to do while we wait you out?" Cary asked. "I'd rather have a nice conversation than just stand here staring at you." To prove her point, she stared at the wizard with her eyes wide, exaggerating the process of staring.

"You're a real bitch, you know that."

"I have heard that before. Usually from assholes like you, so I take it with a grain of salt."

Another wizard bolt hit her shield. The blue light briefly illuminated the dark, narrow street.

Cary took the moment to glance around, still worried about Angie, Marianne, and Lucy. What had happened to them?

Maybe Angie was just keeping everyone out of the way while Cary handled this? Outside of not being able to make the wizard go away, the task of protecting Alan was right in her wheelhouse. This was what she did, all the time, and got paid for. So maybe Angie thought they'd all be safer if they just left Cary to it?

She was about to pull out her cellphone and text them, to make sure nothing else had gone wrong, when a sound from the direction of Cupid Matches caught everyone's attention. Even the wizard turned to look at the storefront.

The neon sign over the door swung. Actually swung. As if a wire had been cut. And was about to fall. Onto the sidewalk.

That wasn't good.

There were no other people around, fortunately, because when the sign hit the sidewalk, it crashed with such a racket, Cary winced. Neon tubes shattered against concrete, spewing shards of glass and metal in a wide swath of destruction.

"What the hell?" the wizard shouted. "How?"

"Sorry about that," a deeper voice from behind them said.

5

<hr>

$\mathcal{C}$ary turned to grin at Angie, who was standing just behind her now. She'd come from the direction where they'd first spotted Alan in trouble and managed to sneak up on them while they'd watched the Cupid Matches sign fall to its sidewalk-induced death.

Angie shrugged. "Well, not really sorry. That place is an abomination."

"Where have you been?" Cary said. "I was worried."

Angie was standing firmly behind Cary now, though, so well within her protection. Which went some way toward making Cary feel better. Still.

"That I am sorry about," Angie said. "I, uh, I touched the building at the corner, got a vision, and realized there were some things the rest of us had to do while you kept the wizard distracted."

"Ah," Cary said as understanding sank in. But also, "Huh?" because she still had a lot of questions.

Angie was a touch psychic and got visions of current and past events when she touched objects and people, sometimes even future events, though that was more ephemeral. Almost always, she had to open to those visions to get them, though. She didn't get hit with one on accident often these days. She'd trained hard to ensure she could control the skill because otherwise, it would make life extremely complicated for her.

Still, it did occasionally happen. So Cary wasn't surprised by that part.

What she really wanted to know was, "What did you do?"

"Broke into the back of the store and freed all the people bound by the wizard's magic."

"Oh." Cary's eyes widened. "Oh wow. Yeah. That was good. And important. Thanks for that."

"No worries. You did a great job keeping the wizard occupied."

"Ah, thanks. Were there a lot of people there?"

"Not in the office, no. Just a lot of bottles holding the binding spells that kept the people controlled. Lucy took out a lot of her anger and frustration at the holiday by breaking them all. Do not get in the way of her angry roundhouse kicks, by the way. Just saying."

Cary chuckled.

"What have you done?" the wizard screeched, so loudly the sound echoed around the narrow street.

"Reset the balance," Angie said.

"Kept you from using innocent people in a very icky way," Cary said. "No more matchmaking for you."

Another series of energy bolts slammed against Cary's shield. She raised her hand in front of her eyes to block out some of the glare.

"So where are Lucy and Marianne now?" Cary asked while the wizard threw magic at them and cursed and screamed.

"There were a couple of people in the back office," Angie said, giving the raging wizard a brief frown. "Once the spells were broken, they were all pretty confused and upset, so Marianne and Lucy are helping them get home."

"In taxis. right?" Cary asked, thinking of all the wine Lucy had been drinking. All the wine they'd all been drinking. It was definitely a leave the car, eat the parking costs, and take a taxi home kind of night.

Although, thanks to doing all this protecting, she was actually fully sober now. The one nice benefit of her job was that she healed fast—

including from hangovers—and she also metabolized alcohol fast if she needed to protect someone.

"In taxis," Angie confirmed. "Marianne and Lucy will join us once they see everyone off."

"Do you realize how much work you've ruined?" the wizard shouted. "How much time and effort you've just destroyed?"

"You were tricking unwilling people into going on dates with your clients," Cary said. "You used magic to manipulate them. And you took away their autonomy in the name of money and…whatever else this got you. I have no sympathy for you. In fact, I think you should be arrested."

"By who? The magic police?" The wizard snorted. "No one was going to be hurt. Everyone got what they wanted—"

"Except the people you had to magic into going on these 'dates'," Cary interrupted.

"And you had no right to interfere," the wizard finished with snarl.

"Of course I did," Cary said. "No consent, no date. That's the rules."

"I'm going to kill you," the wizard said.

"I've heard that one before." Probably more than was good for her long-term survival, honestly. But she didn't think the wizard needed to know that part.

"You're going to be too busy explaining to all your clients what happened," Angie said. To both Cary and the wizard, she said, "Lucy was extra mad, and so we broke into the computer system and sent all the clients an email…explaining things."

"How?" the wizard hissed.

Angie waved her hand. "Hard to hide passwords from a touch psychic."

"Touch psychic?" Alan asked.

"Long story," Cary said. "We'll explain later." Maybe. Depended on if Angie wanted a strange man running around the city knowing she could get visions from touching things. "You told them about the magic stuff?" Cary asked Angie. That didn't sound right.

"No, no," Angie said, "just that Janice here wasn't arranging willing dates for them and that they should demand their money back."

The wizard's name was Janice. Good to know.

"What have you done?" Janice hissed. "Do you know who I work for? What some of them are capable of?" She backed away from Cary and Angie, glancing in both directions as if she expected an attack at that very moment.

"Given some of the immediate replies," Angie said to Cary, ignoring Janice's panicked questions, "I'd say Janice here is in trouble. And going to be dealing with that trouble for…a while."

"Don't tell me I have to protect her now," Cary said with a groan. She hated when she got stuck protecting bad guys from other bad guys.

"I doubt it." Angie finally looked at the wizard. "Got the impression you're resourceful. You'll be able to deal with the…angry ones. Right?"

"Bitch," Janice hissed at Angie.

"Well, actually, in this case, it is witch," Cary corrected.

"You've ruined everything! Cost me everything!"

"I don't feel bad about that," Cary said. "Because you were using people against their will. I'm going to say again, you should find another line of work."

"Also, I would lay low. And maybe leave Portland," Angie said. "Your clients might even forget your betrayal. After a while."

"Some of my clients are powerful, dangerous people," Janice said, her voice low. "This will not end well for you. For any of you."

"I'm not the one they're going to care about," Cary said.

"Initial responses so far," Angie said, "do seem to be focused on what they'll do to *you*."

Janice's eyes took on that wild, glazed look Cary associated with trapped animals. A trapped wizard was as dangerous as any trapped predator. Cary edged Angie a little further behind her and prepared to take the hit when Janice exploded.

But instead of throwing another wizard bolt or even attempting a physical attack, Janice turned in a circle, hunting the street. Then, without another word, she took off, running in her impressively high heels without any trouble.

And wasn't that just irritating.

Cary sighed. "Okay, well, that got rid of her."

"Aren't you going to…go after her? Stop her. Or something?" Alan asked.

Cary turned to face him and Angie. "Not really what we do," Cary said.

"Her clients will take care of her," Angie said. "Don't worry. We… might have let them know she'd run and they'd better move tonight if they wanted compensation."

The way Angie said "compensation" made Cary a little nervous. "Uhm…"

"A refund," Angie said, giving her a reassuring shoulder pat. "I know how you feel about protecting bad guys and didn't want to put you into a position where you felt you'd have to. Especially with this bad guy. She's a nasty piece of work. So we…sort of told her clients where her money was so they could get theirs back."

"Ah, okay." Ensuring the wizard went broke after she'd tried to use people against their will seemed fair enough compensation for crimes committed. Or at least compensation Cary—and Janice for that matter —could live with. "She said some of them were dangerous."

"Well, she catered to unique people, not just mundane humans."

"What's that mean?" Alan asked. "Mundane humans? Unique people?"

"Uhm," Cary said with a slight frown. "You sure you want to know? Once you do, it's hard to go back to living your life without… noticing. Ignorance can be convenient sometimes." Alan had been through a lot already this evening. Cary wasn't sure he needed the extra pressure of knowing the world was not as he thought it was. He'd seen enough of that already.

"More…magic stuff?" he asked, looking between her and Angie.

"Something like that," Angie said.

"'Fraid so," Cary said.

"Yeah, I don't want to know."

"It's better that way." Cary's turn to give a reassuring shoulder pat. "You need help getting back to your car safely?"

"What I could really use is a drink," Alan said on a long sigh.

The fact that he didn't balk at being seen safely to his car by a couple of women raised Cary's opinion of him, an opinion that was already tipped toward him being a decent guy.

"I need another drink too," a high, sweet voice said. Lucy and Marianne rounded the corner. "This killed my buzz and I'm not done being pissed off about Valentine's Day yet," Lucy added as they joined Cary and the others.

"First, you were more than buzzed," Marianne pointed out.

"Second, you did destroy a bunch of property just a few minutes ago," Angie said. "That didn't help with the pissed off thing?"

"It might have helped a little," Lucy admitted with a shrug. "But I miss my buzz." She narrowed her eyes at Marianne, daring her to correct the assessment of her level of drunkenness again.

Marianne raised her hands, palms facing Lucy. "I'm not saying anything."

"Want to join us for a drink and a lot of Valentine's Day complaining?" Cary asked Alan. It was, after all, a rough holiday for a lot of people. And the singles had to stick together.

"We're celebrating Galentine's Day instead," Lucy explained. "Hi, I'm Lucy, by the way."

"Alan." He shook her outstretched hand, still looking faintly bemused by his situation.

Cary introduced Marianne and Angie—since Lucy had made clear Cary had fallen down on the introductions—and then asked, "So what do you say? A little Galentine's Day celebration to make up for a difficult night-before-Valentine's-Day night?"

"I'm not a gal," Alan pointed out, but his mouth ticked up at one side.

"Palentine's Day then," Lucy said. "You can be our new pal." She wove her arm through his and started down the street.

"Buzzed, my ass," Marianne murmured under her breath.

Cary pressed her lips together so she wouldn't laugh.

"Valentine's Day is a crock," Lucy announced. Again. "And we need to oppose it at every turn."

"Uh huh," Alan said, his expression a mix of confusion and amusement as he looked down at Lucy.

"Let me tell you about this scam of a holiday, Alan," Lucy said.

Marianne sighed. "That girl has got to chill out about Valentine's Day."

They fell into step behind Lucy and Alan, heading in the general direction of noise and lights and an area where they could find an open bar.

"We get another bottle of wine into her, she'll be fine," Angie said. "And maybe some Tequila."

Cary glanced back at the remains of the Cupid Matches sign, where it had scattered in sparkling shards of glass across the sidewalk. She hoped that was the end of Janice's forced dates business. But Cary would let her bosses and her faery mentor, Jaxer, know about this later.

Just in case.

"I think we could all use a shot of Tequila after tonight," Cary said.

"Couldn't agree more," Angie said.

"Not going to argue," Marianne said at almost the same time.

She gave them both a shoulder-squeeze hug. "Thanks for your help tonight."

"Never a dull holiday around you, is there?" Angie said.

Marianne snorted. "Never a dull holiday around any of you."

Cary grinned. "Happy Galentine's Day!"

CARY'S LEPRECHAUN TROUBLES

Because of course leprechaun trouble on St. Patrick's Day…

When magical Protector Cary Redmond's mentor asks for her help, she finds herself in a grocery store parking lot on a beautiful spring day. Staring at the best dressed leprechaun she's ever seen. And since that leprechaun irritates her mentor a lot, Cary decides this mission could be fun.

The trouble the leprechaun brings with him…not so fun.

Saving the day, finding an ancient relic, preventing the bad guys from driving all humankind into the sea… What better way to spend St. Patrick's Day.

So long as she can manage to hold off the deadly plot without anyone getting killed.

1

———————

*C*ary stared at the leprechaun. The leprechaun stared back.

A leprechaun who needed help on St. Patrick's Day was… Well, it was a thing. And probably she shouldn't have been surprised, given the last few years of her life.

Still, finding herself facing a leprechaun in the parking lot of a grocery store in a residential suburb of Portland was a strange enough experience it gave her pause.

The leprechaun was a handsome man, decked out in the nicest suit she'd ever seen on anyone in real life, tailored perfectly to his smaller size, and showing off a nicely fit physique. Dark gray suit, crisp white shirt underneath, and a green tie with shamrocks on it. The tie was probably a little inside joke, but she didn't really get it. He had long, dark brown hair pulled back into a low tail, and his green eyes glimmered with mischief.

His grin was exactly the kind of grin that normally spelled Trouble in her life.

She flicked a glance between her mentor and the leprechaun. "You're sure about this?" she asked Jaxer while still staring at the leprechaun he'd introduced at Tom.

Jaxer was a faery, an unreally gorgeous blond man who she suspected toned down his looks with his best magic—glamour. He was her mentor in her job as a magical Protector, which she'd been doing for a couple of years now. And with great frequency, he was a very large pain in her ass.

At the moment, though, she was more interested in what a pain in the ass the leprechaun was for Jaxer.

To say she wasn't amused by all this would be a blatant lie. Jaxer could be so frustratingly annoying when he put his mind to it, it was pretty fun to watch him get some of that back. The animosity between him and Tom was very nearly a physical thing. And she suspected that if Jaxer didn't consider this trouble Very Serious, he wouldn't have agreed to any of this in the first place.

Still, she did feel the need to make sure Jaxer was absolutely certain this was necessary.

"He's not likely to tell you the truth," the leprechaun said. "Ye know that, right?"

"Of course I tell her the truth." Jaxer scowled at the shorter man. "She's my mentee."

"Ah, because the English are so good with the truth, are they then?"

Jaxer snarled.

Cary pressed her lips together so she wouldn't laugh. Jaxer, apparently, had ties to both the English and the Irish Fae courts, but he'd never seen fit to tell her exactly how he was connected to both. In fact, he never talked about the European Fae courts at all except in vague terms. Like her, he worked for—or with? She wasn't sure. But she thought for—a group of North American Fae, the Fae that created Protectors like her. And any details about his life in the Old World got brushed off with vague hand waving.

She did notice his accent swung between an Irish lilt and an English snootiness depending on who he was talking to, though. Little more Irish with her and their bosses. Little more English right now with the leprechaun.

Which was fascinating. And if they didn't have someone to protect in that very moment, she'd have just let the conversation continue so she could hopefully learn some juicy secrets about her mentor.

But, according to Jaxer, and Tom for that matter, there wasn't much time.

"If you're certain about this, shouldn't we…you know, get to it, then?" she asked the two scowling Fae. "I was under the impression there was some, uh, urgency?"

Tom didn't know Cary was a Protector—she didn't go around telling people that for her own safety, and Jaxer had warned her especially not to reveal her true job description to Tom. To Tom, she was a witch with some really great shielding powers and Jaxer was training her in different ways to use her magic.

Technically, that was almost true. Jaxer was training her. And she did have some really great shields. But the power for those shields came from her Fae bosses, she just channeled it. And shielding was pretty much all she did. She had no natural magic of her own, and no way to actually *do* anything. But she could get between bad guys and good guys and keep the good guys safe until the end of days.

Her favorite analogy for her job was that she was a walking, talking Kevlar vest. She could even stop bullets. Though if she had to leap between the bullet and an innocent person when the bullet was already moving, she tended to get hit. Just not killed. Still. The pinpoint cracks in her ribs and the weird bruising were *really* hard to explain to the Emergency Room people.

"There is, indeed, some level of urgency," Tom said. "And I'd be grateful to yer man here if he'd stop wasting our time."

"I'm not the one wasting time," Jaxer huffed. "We're here, aren't we? I can't follow the damned rainbow."

Cary raised her brows. There was so much about this she didn't understand. Jaxer had just said an asshole leprechaun needed there help and they needed to hurry. He'd given her this address, said he'd met her here, and twenty minutes later, here they were. In a parking lot. A surprisingly empty parking lot, despite it being the middle of the day.

With two stubborn members of the Fae, just glaring at each other rather than actually explaining *why* they were here. Or even just getting on with things.

"Rainbow?" she asked, looking around the lot. There were a few cars parked at the opposite end of the lot, and a shopping cart that hadn't been returned to the cart rack turned on its side a few yards away. Trees leading into a small park behind the grocery store bracketed the lot—that's where Jaxer had reappeared from after she'd pulled into the lot. But no rainbows.

She frowned at Jaxer. "I thought that rainbow thing was…uhm, not true?" She glanced at Tom. The pot of gold at the end of the rainbow was one of those things she'd learned, after becoming a Protector, was a myth that didn't have a basis in reality. Since she hadn't realized leprechauns were real before becoming a Protector, she'd never considered the rainbow thing one way or the other.

"Yer right there, missus," Tom said with a charming grin. "The stories you tell about us aren't precisely true. But there're basis to all myths. And this one… Well, there's a bit of a truth to parts of it."

"Cool," she said. "Do I get to find out what that truth is or…no?"

Tom chuckled. "Depends. If you're nice, I might tell you."

"Flirting? Really?"

"Sure and why not?"

"I could be dangerous," she said, trying to maintain a serious expression. She wasn't even a little dangerous. Just stubborn and better at running into trouble than running away from it. But dangerous was…not her thing.

"Is that supposed to deter me?" Tom asked with a little smile.

"Enough," Jaxer said, scowling at them both.

She gave Jaxer a look. He sounded extremely irritated. She should probably stop encouraging Tom to irritate Jaxer—even though she wasn't entirely sure what in this exchange bugged Jaxer. She didn't know if Tom was in the good guy category or the bad guy category yet. Jaxer had been pretty cagey on that point. But watching her unrufflable mentor being ruffled by the leprechaun was delightful.

"You asked for my help," Jaxer said to Tom. "Get on with it."

"Sure and I wouldn't have asked if I'd known you'd be such an ass about it."

"Why did you ask?" Cary interjected. If they were this antagonistic toward each other, Tom coming to Jaxer for help seemed…unusual.

Tom snarled. "He was close."

"If you thought I'd be anything but an ass when you contacted me," Jaxer said, "you were deluding yourself."

"You'll thank me afterward."

"Me thank *you*?"

"Boys," Cary said into the growing argument as the two of them got into each other's faces. "Don't we have something to do? Something I'm still clueless about. And could use a clue, by the way."

Not that it mattered to her powers. She didn't have to know what she was facing, what sort of situation she was getting into the middle of. She just needed to get between good guys and bad guys and her magic went up and the good guys were safe. That was the theory anyway. So far, the magic had never failed her.

She did worry sometimes…actually, a lot, that someday the magic would fail, and she'd get someone killed. But so far, that hadn't happened. And the longer she did this, the more she trusted the Protector powers.

Still, she was nosey, and she really wanted to know what was going on.

"This way then," Tom said. To Jaxer, he added, "If yer done pissing around."

"Fuck off," Jaxer said.

Tom grinned. Then turned and headed toward the trees at the side of the parking lot.

Cary glanced at Jaxer. Jaxer scowled after Tom, but nodded. And they both followed the leprechaun.

Cary leaned close and asked, "What are we getting into here?"

Jaxer sighed. "Just…stay between us and whatever happens. It's St. Patrick's Day and Tom's called *me* for help. What's on the other side of this transition will be bad."

"Wait. You don't know?"

Before he could answer, they stepped into the trees, Cary swore she saw the flickering of colorful rainbow lights at the edge of her vision, and then they were somewhere…

Not a grocery store parking lot.

2

"Where the hell are we?" Cary asked, glancing around.

They were surrounded by tall trees, mostly pine with a few oaks thrown in. Bright blue sky overhead. Cool spring breeze blowing through the trees. A few twittering birds. The pine smell was lovely, but the fact that they weren't in the city anymore, that she could hear the ocean in the distance, and that she might have forgotten to lock her car door, left her a little disoriented and irritable.

Jaxer grinned at her. "I thought you liked nature walks."

She scowled. Back to the order of things. Her being irritated while Jaxer grinned. The universal balance restored. "You could have warned me," she hissed.

"Where would be the fun in that?"

She rolled her eyes. "What happened? Why am I low level nauseous? Where are we?"

Tom stood a few feet away, looking around the base of a huge spruce pine. "We're a few miles from the Pacific," he said, "still here in Oregon. And we're looking for something."

"Okay." She glanced around. "That missed the how and the why I'm nauseous, but at least the where was answered."

"Leprechaun trick," Jaxer said. "Transition gate. The rainbow."

"Huh?"

"Not all of us can manage it," Tom said, still not looking at her as he hunted around the base of the tree. "But with the right bit of gold, we can work a little gate that takes us where we need to go while avoiding moving through Faery."

"Oh. That's…good." Very good because moving through Faery was extremely dangerous for humans. And she was a human. Very very human. Jaxer had warned her a long time ago to never enter Faery. She'd taken that warning to heart. "Avoiding moving through Faery is good. How does the rainbow gate thing work?"

"Like I said," Tom muttered from behind the tree. "Right bit of gold, touch of magic, very skilled leprechaun."

Jaxer rolled his eyes at Tom's last comment.

"I thought…" She frowned at Jaxer. "Don't you guys go into and through Faery all the time?"

"We do," Tom answered. "But sometimes, it's best not."

"And why is he avoiding Faery?" Cary asked Jaxer, leaning in close and hoping Tom wouldn't hear.

"Probably pissed someone off," Jaxer grumbled.

Tom poked his head around the base of the huge tree and winked. Then disappeared again.

"What are you looking for?" Cary called.

"If I can find it before they get here," Tom said, "it'll make things a lot easier."

"That… That didn't answer my question." And also, "They who?"

A low rumbling answered her. The ground beneath her feet shivered and started to vibrate. A sound like the sliding of metal against metal rose from the soil, making her wince.

She circled slowly, looking for the source of the noises, putting Jaxer and Tom at her back so she could protect them from…

"Oh," she said, swallowing hard.

As the first huge snake heads started popping up out of the ground.

"That must be 'they'," she said.

"Ah, shite," Tom muttered as he came around the tree. "Was hoping I'd have a few more minutes. I can't find the damned thing."

More snake heads appeared, followed by waves of snake bodies, as Cary's heartbeat raced. She was a biologist by training, and while snakes weren't her favorite beasties, she wasn't terrified of them. Just respectful of their possible poisonousness or constricting strength. Animals that could potentially kill you deserved respect.

But she'd never seen anything quite like these snakes before.

To start, they weren't normally sized. They were huge. Their heads the size of her basset hound, shaped a bit like a cobra in a rough triangle, topped with red eyes instead of the a more normal black. And their forked tongues, when flickering out to taste the air, were easily three feet long.

Green and black scales slid through the earth and rocks, creating that metal against metal sound. The scales didn't look like they were made of metal, but they were slightly pebbled so maybe they were more boney than normal scales? The snakes themselves weren't normal with those red eyes, so the actual biology was…up for grabs.

She couldn't count exactly how many of them there were, but she guessed at least five or six. It was hard to tell the way they ungulated through the ground, rising up and then sinking back beneath the soil like it was water, churning up rich dirt and pine needles. She couldn't begin to tell how long their bodies were, but she'd guess pretty long based on the size of their heads.

"What the hell kind of snakes are those?" she asked, even as she put herself more solidly between the danger and her companions. If she was protecting the two Fae, the snakes couldn't hurt them. And the snakes couldn't hurt her. Which was a nice bonus to her job. While protecting someone, she was pretty much indestructible—except for the occasional bruise and broken bone, of course.

"Not normal," Tom said.

She huffed and glanced over her shoulder at him. "Really? The glowing red eyes didn't give that away at all. I would never have guessed."

Tom snorted. "I didn't think Americans understood sarcasm. Glad to see ye have it in you."

"Sure sure. Gonna explain the snakes, or are we just going to stand here and watch them slither around?"

The snakes had stopped a few feet away, rising their heads farther out of the soil. One ducked back down into the dirt and a moment later, she heard Tom gasp. She glanced back to see one of the beasties high out of the ground, its head a foot from Tom, it's forked tongue looking a little smashed against its nose.

"What…?" Tom stared at the snake. "Why isn't it…?"

"Oh, sorry, right, I've got that part," Cary said. "You're safe. Just stay behind me."

Tom looked at her, eyebrows raised.

She shrugged. "Good shields." And that was all he needed to know.

"Fair enough." He looked back at the snake as it swung away from him and back down into the soil.

A little bump against the ground under her feet made Cary's eyes widen. She looked down. Nothing rose up under her, but a moment later, she watched green and black scales rise out of the dirt, flowing from beneath her. She was pretty sure one of those snakes had just tried to get at her from beneath.

And wasn't that just a little terrifying.

"Can't just sneak up on me," she told the snakes, trying to sound calm but pretty sure Jaxer would hear the squeak in her voice since he knew her so well.

More snake heads rose up around them. Definitely more than five or six now. And not just the giant snakes anymore. All kinds of snakes starting slithering through the soil, churning it like the white water on a river. The entire ground just outside her shield seemed to be moving, and through all that dirt movement, snake bodies rose and fell from view.

So many snakes. Sliding over each other, through and around each other, a constant flow that made here dizzy.

She blinked a few times. "This is wild," she murmured. "Probably not good either, huh?"

"Nope," Jaxer said, moving up closer to her shoulder. "You okay?" he whispered near her ear.

"Great. Great. Love snakes. Well, not really. But not normally terrified of them either. Healthy respect normally. Pretty cool animal. Except this is…a lot of snakes." She swallowed hard.

She knew they were all safe. Her Protector powers were obviously working because there was a good two feet circumference around them that was entirely snake free. And Tom hadn't been eaten by that one that tried to sneak up on him.

Still, knowing they were safe and her powers were working was only a little reassuring when surrounded by literally thousands of snakes just beyond that two-foot gap of safety.

"Still waiting to hear the plan," she called back to Tom. "And, you know, maybe an explanation. That might be nice. Not to nag or anything." Although, she absolutely could if needs be. She'd inherited a great nagging gene from her mother.

"I need to find the staff," Tom said. "Before they get here."

"They?" She gave the writhing mass of snakes a look, then glanced back at the leprechaun. "I thought *they* were already here. We're expecting more snakes? Or someone not a snake? Or…?"

Wouldn't really matter who "they" were, because the threat didn't matter to her shield. They were safe and would stay safe no matter who showed up. Still, she kind of hoped for some advanced notice, seeing as how the snakes had been something of a shock. She'd had enough of those for one day.

She glanced up at the bright blue sky. For some reason, this felt like the sort of thing that should be happening at night. Lots of weird paranormal stuff happened at night. The middle of a sunny, gorgeous day with hints of spring in the air felt…wrong for weird snake activity.

She studied more of the smaller snakes. They didn't seem to have the red eyes of the larger ones. But they outnumbered the larger snakes by…well, she couldn't tell. From her vantage, it looked like a thousand to one. But since it was impossible to pick out individual snake bodies in the tangle, she didn't actually have a clue.

"These aren't…" She leaned back and lowered her voice so only

Jaxer would hear—she didn't want Tom to realize how much she didn't know. She'd been studying for more than three years now and she still felt like she knew absolutely nothing. "Are those Nagas?" she whispered.

The snake shifters were notoriously reclusive, living in their own cities in realms attached to this one but not part of it. She'd never seen a Naga in real life before, so she didn't know what they looked like. But the huge size of the red-eyed snakes made her think of snake shifters.

"Not Nagas," Jaxer said, his voice a very quiet murmur next to her ear. "Not shapeshifters of any kinds. Real snakes. Or, well, magic snakes. The big ones. Just not snakes that change shapes."

"Cool. Thanks." She gave his arm a little pat, and he gave her a slight grin and a wink. Having her mentor *with* her while she was working a job was unusual, so it was nice to have him on hand to actually ask questions. Usually, she had to save up all her questions for after the job.

Although, to be fair, he'd gotten her into this job. As far as she knew, this wasn't something her bosses had assigned her to do.

"Still waiting on the explanation for all this," she called back to Tom as Jaxer took a few steps away.

"I'm looking for the damned staff. Give me a minute."

She glanced back to see Tom once again climbing around the huge base of the spruce tree, up onto thick, heavy roots, poking at the bark. The scent of pine sap filled the air, a nice contrast to that dryish reptilian smell surrounding them. Not that all the snakes smelled bad. Snakes had a distinct kind of smell, but it wasn't bad. They didn't stink like some mammals did. But there were just so many of them, all around, that the scent was strong. And so was the pervasiveness of churned soil.

Actually, if it weren't for the danger—whatever it actual was; no one had seen fit to explain anything yet—she'd have liked the very earthy, spring, piney scent surrounding them. Might have even enjoyed a hike in these trees. But… Snakes.

"Any idea what he's looking for?" she asked Jaxer since Tom didn't seem to be very forthcoming with the information.

"Given the snakes," Jaxer said, "if I had to guess. I'd say the Staff of St. Patrick."

3

ary blinked a few times at her mentor. Then blinked some more at the snakes. "Huh?"

"You know, St. Patrick?" Jaxer said. "The guy who drove the snakes from Ireland? Whole reason for the St. Patrick's Day celebrations."

"Oh yeah." The holiday wasn't just about beer and corned beef and dying rivers green. Who knew?

"Ye know we don't eat corned beef in Ireland, right?" Tom asked from behind the giant spruce.

Had he read her mind? "What do you eat?"

"Ham. The good stuff. Corned beef is a poor man's ham."

"Okay." That was interesting, actually. And something she'd like to talk more to him about. After they got out from in the middle of all the snakes, of course.

"Can we get back to the staff, though?" she asked. "I mean…are you talking a literal staff owned by an old Irish saint, or is that just a metaphoric name for some magical device?"

"Yes," Tom said.

She scowled at Jaxer. Jaxer gave her a look she interpreted as, "I warned you he was an ass." Which technically, Jaxer hadn't, but his opinion of the leprechaun had been pretty obvious from the start.

"Not helpful," she told Tom.

"It's a magical staff," Tom said, sounding irritated, "that happened to have been used by the old Irish guy who went on to become a saint for driving all them snakes off the island. The snakes weren't natural to the island to begin with. Magical mess got them there. And this old fella was given the staff to help fix the problem."

"Old fella?" she mouthed at Jaxer.

"Patrick," he mouthed back.

Thinking of the saint whose name had been given to the holiday as just Patrick felt weird. But she supposed before he was a saint, he was a normal man, right? Just…strange to think about.

"I thought St. Patrick got the snakes out of Ireland using…God or something. Thus the saint part of St. Patrick."

She wasn't actually clear on the finer points, though. To her, St. Patrick's Day was beer and corned beef—even though apparently the corned beef part was wrong. But she thought, since old Patrick had become a Catholic saint, that there was some link to Catholicism and God in there somewhere. At least in the stories most people knew.

"Sure and wasn't that what he told the other monks," Tom said. "Wouldn't do to say he'd gotten a magical staff from Faery and used it, now would it? Too pagan and superstitious, even though those old fellas were rightly superstitious."

She wasn't sure what to say to any of that, but she was fascinated. "The staff is something out of Faery?"

That had to mean it was dangerous, right? Everything from Faery was dangerous. And she included her mentor in that camp. She liked Jaxer a lot. He'd become a good friend. But that made him no less dangerous.

She considered the fact that her powers came through Fae bosses and that, technically, they could be considered dangerous. But since all she was able to do with them was…stand here and keep dangerous things out, calling the magic she channeled dangerous felt like some sort of oxymoron.

Huh. She'd have to think about that more. But at the moment, she was certain that any physical object like this staff coming out of Faery had to mean it wasn't exactly a safe-to-handle sort of thing.

The snakes seemed to be writhing faster now, the soil churning so much it was a carpet of movement without any solid spaces left. Every inch of earth under the trees and around them pulsed with movement.

"Got a feeling something's about to happen," she said, her voice pitched for both Jaxer and Tom. "Might want to hurry up with the staff, if that's what we need here."

"You think I'm just picking my nose up in this tree?" Tom snapped.

"Well…" Jaxer said.

Cary scowled at him. "Hush. Don't make things worse." To Tom she called, "Not trying to rush you. We're good. Take your time."

Panicking someone who was trying to find something only made things worse. She knew this from first-hand experience as both the panicker and the panickee. Or…person doing the panicking? She shook her head. She'd have to work out the word semantics later. Right now, she had snakes to keep out.

Not that she was required to do more than stand here. Still, she wanted to concentrate. Just in case.

A spot a few feet outside of her shield, in the center of the writhing mass, started to lift, like a strange soil volcano, rising and writhing and spilling soil and snakes down the sides. It was weird and spooky, and Cary was quite certain this was that something she'd been worried about.

Maybe the mysterious "they" Tom had been referring to?

"Jaxer…" Cary said, her tone half warning, half urgency.

"I'll help Tom," he said.

"Good idea." She couldn't look away from the snake and dirt volcano. "I'll just…stand here and make sure we're all safe. Don't move outside of my…shield."

"I'm the one who taught you that, you know," Jaxer said, dryly.

"There's a snake volcano that's almost as tall as me just a few feet away. We can argue about word choice in terrifying emergency situations later."

"Fecker's around here somewhere," Tom muttered. "Jaxer, get yer arse over here and help me look."

She felt more than saw Jaxer move back to the spruce because she was too busy staring at the snake volcano. It was taller than her now, which meant she had to tilt her head back to look at the tip of it. Another foot of dirt and snakes climbed upward before the whole thing started to collapse. Snakes and dirt alike falling like a waterfall back down to the ground.

Revealing four leprechauns standing on the shoulders of one another, making a pole of leprechauns.

She blinked a few times, staring at them. The three on the bottom where all wearing fancy suits and ties, which were remarkably clean given they'd just been rising up through soil and snakes. The leprechaun at the top of the stack, wore an actual gown, a fancy green gown like the sort of thing someone might wear walking a red carpet. The dress-wearing leprechaun had her hair done up in an elaborate series of braids stacked on top of her head. And slithering around those braids, one very slim black snake. With red eyes.

The others lower in the stack also had one tiny black snake with red eyes sliding through their fancy hairstyles. All four leprechauns had hair on the long side, decorated in braids and the single snake. All four leprechauns also had strangely colored eyes. Like a mix of red and green that came out a bit muddy but muddy in a way that glowed.

Cary gave her head a hard shake.

Huh. "I have no idea what to make of this, but we got four more leprechauns dressed up beautifully and with snakes in their hair." She called this over her shoulder without looking away from the newcomers.

"We've come for the staff," the top leprechaun intoned. She had a beautiful voice, strong and resonate. The snake slithered over her head, through her braids, and across her forehead almost like a diadem.

Cary waited for them to separate and the top leprechauns to jump off the shoulders of the person beneath them, but they stayed as they were in a stack.

Okay. "Out of curiosity," she said, "what do you need the staff for?

I mean…" She gestured at the snakes. "I'm seeing a lot of snakes here, but I'm assuming they're with you, so you don't want to drive them out or anything. And given the snakes in your hair and, again, all the snakes present here in these woods, I'm also assuming you don't need the staff to control snakes. So… Why dig up—so to speak—old St. Patrick's staff?"

"Not his," hissed the top leprechaun. "Alwaysss ourssss."

"Lot of sibilant Ss going on there," Cary said. "Very snaky. I like it. Seems appropriate. But doesn't answer my question."

"The ssstaff is ourssss."

"Yeah, no. I'm going to say it's not because you having it seems like a bad idea." Even if she didn't know what their ultimate reason for wanting the thing was.

"You can't ssstop us." Still from the leprechaun at the top of the stack. But now all four of them started to move in a sort of undulating wave, like a snake rising out of a basket or something.

If they lunged forward and tried to strike like a snake, Cary was definitely going to scream. "Actually," she said, swallowing her own fear, "that's exactly what I do. Stop people. Well, stop bad guys. And I'm betting that, in this instant, you're the bad guys. Though I'd love to have someone enlighten me on why and to what end?" She gestured at the snakes. "What's this all for?"

"To drive them out?"

"The snakes?"

"The people."

Ah. That…didn't sound good.

4

"Found what you're looking for yet?" Cary called back to Tom and Jaxer where she assumed they were still crawling around the spruce tree. The stack of four leprechauns standing in front of her, undulating like a huge snake, was impossible to look away from, so she couldn't actually see what Toma and Jaxer were doing.

They didn't answer her, though there was some cursing and a few snippy comments between faery and leprechaun.

"Press that part," Tom snapped.

"I did," Jaxer snapped back. "You tired there?"

"Twice, ye gobshite. You're missing an entire section."

"You're missing that bit over there."

Since the two men were ignoring her, Cary went back to trying to get answers from the leprechaun stack. She wasn't sure how to think of them. They were definitely four individuals, but seemed to be working as a single unit like they were one individual, so she supposed she should address them that way? She'd have liked to ask Jaxer more, since he was actually here. But he was busy. So, she'd have to wait.

"So…" she said as the undulating leprechauns approached the edge of her shield. "Why drive all the people out? And, uh, where would they go?"

"Into the sea," the leprechauns all said at once, all four voices blending like music.

Weirdest Greek chorus ever. "All the people? Into the sea?"

"They did it to us."

"Uhm, I'm not sure that's right…?" But since she wasn't entirely sure what was happening, she couldn't be certain. Obviously, it wasn't the leprechauns driven into the sea by St. Patrick. That was snakes. Supposedly. And, really, up until this very moment, she'd been convinced it was also just a myth, a story.

Since there was a real staff, and had apparently been a real monk named Patrick who used it, and it obviously did have to do with snakes, she had to assume the story was real-ish. But what did all this have to do with leprechauns? And why were the leprechauns working with red-eyed snakes? And what *were* the red-eyed snakes?

Lot of questions she could have asked Jaxer if he wasn't busy trying to find the very staff in question.

"We have waited long to take our revenge," the four leprechauns said at once.

"Sure sure. But still not getting the connection here."

"Got it!" Tom shouted from the pine tree.

"Oh good."

Because the leprechaun stack finally reached the edge of her shield and were pressing against it, searching for a way past. There wasn't a way past. But the fact that they were trying creeped her out. She was a little worried what might happen if those red-eyed snakes got too close. The little ones in the leprechauns' hair worried her more than the oversized ones still moving though the rest of the writhing mass of snakes and soil like giant sea monsters moving through a school of fish.

Tom and Jaxer stepped up on either side of her, but when Tom would have stepped in front of her, she put a hand out and held him back. "Stay behind me," she warned. "Only way I can keep you safe." She flicked at glance at him when she felt his gaze on the side of her face. "It's how my shield works, okay? Don't mess it up. Unless you want to be instantly surrounded by snakes."

"Prefer not to," Tom said. "Yer right there. Specially those buggers with the red eyes."

"Yeah, been wondering about them."

"We will have our revenge," the four leprechauns said at once.

"Friends of yours?" Cary asked.

"Used to be. Used to be." He sounded so resigned, she glanced down at him again. He gave her a little shrug. "Red-eyed beasties got to them. Not sure the staff will bring them back. Might be lost to us. And that would be a damned shame."

"Yeah it would." She frowned. "They're not doing this on purpose? The red-eyed snakes are…manipulating them?"

"They are." Tom sighed. "And we've found nothing that can break the spell."

"Except for the staff?"

"The staff was supposed to remain hidden," Tom said. "Out of their reach." He winced and wouldn't look up at her when he said, "I'm breaking with the leadership, if you like, here. Gone rogue."

"To save your friends? That's so sweet."

"Don't get soft on him," Jaxer said. "He's probably doing it for pay, not sentimentality."

"You doing this for pay?" she asked Tom.

"There might be some coin at the end of this rainbow," Tom allowed.

She rolled her eyes at the rainbow comment.

"But I'd be doing the deed for a lot less than I'm being paid," Tom said. "No way for the lads to go out."

Cary didn't miss his very slight shiver. She could understand. She wouldn't want to be manipulated and controlled by red-eyed snakes either. Even if she had no idea what the red-eyed snakes were and how they were managing all this.

Magic. It had to be magic because that seemed to be the answer to all the weird shit in her life these days. Well, magic or some sort of preternatural beastie, like a shapeshifter or a vampire. Or demons. Sometimes it was demons.

Her life had gotten really weird in the last few years.

But red-eyed snakes controlling leprechauns and looking to send all the humans into the sea was a new one.

"How does the staff work?" she asked as the stack of mind-controlled leprechauns continue to push at the edge of her shield.

"According to the old stories, you hold it up and ask whichever old gods ye worship to give you a hand driving out the snakes."

"Really?" She turned a little to more fully face Tom.

She didn't have to be facing bad guys directly for her shield to keep working. So long as she had someone technically in her protection and behind her—metaphorically speaking since she could wrap her arms around someone and achieve the same effect—her shields worked. She liked to keep the bad guys in her line of sight because she didn't like surprises and bad guys tended to do jumping, scary thing when you weren't looking. But keeping the bad guys in sight wasn't, technically, required.

"The staff works by just appealing to some god and...hoping they listen?"

"Na, that's just the old stories," Tom said, with a little head shake. "Didn't I just say that?"

She scowled. "Are you stalling and wasting time because you don't *know* how the staff works?"

"Told you she was smart," Jaxer said, sounding smug.

She preened at the compliment.

Tom rolled his eyes. "It's been hidden away for centuries," he said. "And I'm no monk."

Jaxer snorted a rude laugh.

"But I know the theory," Tom finished, ignoring Jaxer.

"Which is?" Cary asked.

"Right so." Tom raised the staff and gave it a little shake.

Cary glanced at the still writhing mass of snakes in the ground around them, the red-eyed snakes still sliding across the foreheads of the four leprechauns who were all, still and amazingly, standing one on top of the other's shoulders, pressing at different points in her shield.

"Not working yet," she said.

"Haven't gotten started yet, have I?" Tom snapped. "Just warming up."

"Sure sure. No hurry. Take your time." She wasn't being sarcastic. They actually did have all the time Tom needed so long as the leprechauns and the snakes stayed focused on their little group and didn't try to wander off and drive people into the sea without the staff.

Which would be bad.

"Anything you can do in the meantime?" She leaned close to Jaxer again. "Give them something to play with? Keep them occupied until Tom gets that staff figured out?"

"He will never control the staff," the four leprechauns said in unison.

Cary shivered. "That's creepy when you all do that, you know?"

"The staff is ours to control. We will have it back."

She sighed. "I'm going to say no to that, because…not everyone can swim and people aren't adapted to living in the sea—"

"We know. That's the point."

So hard not to roll her eyes at that comment. "So—" she emphasized the word, "—I'm not letting any humans to be driven into the sea. Thanks very much."

"You cannot stop us."

"Hear that a lot," she said, with a little head tilt. "Lots of people tell me I can't stop them and then I stop them. It's a real shock to the system, I have to tell you. You might want to prepare now."

"We will not be stopped," the leprechauns roared and there was a surge of snakes at her shield.

They all came up hard against the barrier. Hissing and some colorful leprechaun curses followed.

"See?" she said. "Stopped. Now, do you want to be reasonable and talk about this, or are you just going to keep throwing yourselves at my shield?"

More snakes flew at her shield.

She shook her head. "Such a waste of energy. You know, you could always tell me how the staff works. I figure you have a clue since you're here to get it and everything. I'm really curious. I didn't even know such a thing existed."

"It is ours to control! We will not be denied."

"She's good at pissing 'em off and keeping 'em distracted," Tom whispered around her back to Jaxer.

"The best," Jaxer said with an approving nod.

He patted Cary one the shoulder and she preened again. It was nice to know her mentor thought she was doing well in her job.

"Any epiphanies with the staff?" she asked Tom.

"I've got it. Any moment now."

"Fair enough. Keep trying." She went back to the snakes. "So… Any reason you have for now, after all this time, wanting to send humans into the sea? Oh, and what are you, exactly? Not the leprechauns, I mean I know what you are, of course. But I'm more thinking the snakes with the red-eyes. You want to clarify who…what you are? Cause I'm really curious. And since I know you're not Nagas, and probably not any kind of snake shifter…?" She glanced at Jaxer.

Jaxer shook his head.

"Okay, so not snake shifters. What would you be then?"

She wasn't expecting answers. She just rambled as a way to keep the snakes and leprechauns distracted and focused on her. If they were concentrating on trying to get through her shield and irritated by her efforts at asking questions, they would not be focused on trying to stop Tom while he figured out how to get the staff to work.

She did give the staff a few quick looks from the corner of her eye, a little surprised it was so ordinary given it was *the* staff that had helped Patrick drive the snakes from Ireland. It was also Fae, and Fae stuff tended to be bejeweled and glittery and…ostentatious. Like Jaxer. Jaxer was always ostentatious with his silk shirts left unbuttoned too much to show off his chest no matter what the weather. He did have a nice chest, to be fair to him, but still. He never got cold?

Speaking of which, a cold breeze shifted through the trees as the sun changed positions and dropped the wooded area deeper into shadows. This time of year, the weather could be a little hit or miss. Lovely and almost warm, but mostly wet and cold. The fact that it was cold but still sunny was actually a lovely combination. But she did pull her leather jacket tighter around her to keep out the colder wind.

"Got it!" Tom announced suddenly.

All the snakes and leprechauns froze in that instant, turning in a weird unison to stare at Tom. He gulped, audibly, and stepped a little farther behind her.

"What do you need to do?" Cary asked, trying to pull his attention from all the red eyes staring at him now.

He raised the staff, spun it in a small circle above his head, then gripped it with both hands and brought it back down hard into the soil.

Because Cary was watching the snakes closer than she was watching Tom, the sudden surge of *more* snakes did not go unnoticed.

"Uhm," she said. "There are more snakes now. Lots of them."

There'd already been a seething mass of them, but now they were coming up out of the ground and carpeting the forest floor, the number so immense she couldn't even see the soil around them anymore. Not churning dirt now, no. Just a ground made up of snakes.

This was really bad.

5

The writhing snakes piled up against the edge of Cary's shield, around the feet of the leprechaun on the bottom of the four-leprechaun stack, going all the way up to his knees. The hissing sound was like nothing Cary had ever heard, worse than nails on a chalkboard to her nerves. Up to this point, outside of the red-eyed snakes, she hadn't really been able to see the individuals among all the mass of slithering bodies, but now, she watched actual cobras and rattle snakes coming up out of the piles. They struck at the shield in lightning-fast burst, as if they could sting the shield away.

Cary's healthy respect for snakes was starting to turn into downright fear. If those poisonous snakes slipped past her defenses, they were all dead.

"The shield will hold," Jaxer said against her ear. "You know it will."

"Yeah. Sure. But…rattlesnakes. Cobras. Not my favorite animals."

"What are your favorite animals?" Jaxer asked, sounding generally curious. "I didn't think you had a favorite."

She had a soft spot for most animals—typical human she was more drawn to other mammals, but she even found fish and reptiles pretty cool. Favorite? Did she have a favorite? She officially had three dogs in her pack now. But considering two of them weren't normal dogs, just hanging out in normal dog shapes, she wasn't sure that counted as "dogs" being her favorite animal. There was the stray cat Scratchy. But he didn't like her enough for her to consider him her favorite animal.

Huh? She had no idea. She'd have to think about that a little more.

And, she acknowledged, the distraction helped her growing panic a lot. Because the snakes were staying safely outside her shield and she was thinking about which animals she liked best instead of hyperventilating.

"Thanks," she said to Jaxer.

"No problem." He grinned at her, a smug expression that made her groan.

"If you two are done with the mutual appreciation party," Tom said, "we've a wee problem here."

"Called more snakes instead of driving them away with that staff, huh." Cary nodded. "Any idea how to…reverse that?" She twirled a finger over her head. "Maybe do what you just did but backward?"

"That's… That's not how magic works, ye know. You do know that, right?"

"Sure sure. Just a suggestion." She waved a hand at him. "You're the expert."

"The only thing he's an expert at is being a pain in my ass," Jaxer said.

"Not seeing much help over here from the arrogant faery, now am I?" Tom muttered. "Maybe get off yer arse and do something to help besides standing there like a lump."

"Lump?" Jaxer scowled and started to move around Cary.

Cary put an arm out to block him. "Staying behind me. Remember. And he's right. You've got magic. Do something…distracting while he figures out the staff."

The snakes were piling even higher now. They'd nearly covered the leprechaun at the base of the four-leprechaun stack. If Cary hadn't watched them emerge from a soil and snake volcano, she'd be a little worried about that one suffocating.

To Tom, she said, "Maybe there's a button on the staff."

"A button? Ye think this kind of thing comes with buttons?"

"What do I know? I'm not a monk either." Although, given the state of her dating life over the last few years, she might as well be. But that wasn't something she was going to discuss with either Tom or Jaxer. "There's got to be a trick to it, right? Maybe you should call on a god or someone, like the old stories."

"Ye never call on the old gods," Tom said with a hard scowl. "You might get what you ask for. And bolloxed in the process. No old gods. Better off without fretting the gods period."

"Fair enough." What did she know about gods. "Any other bright ideas? I've thrown out a couple and all you do is shoot them down. Let's hear your impressive opinion."

"Better opinions than yours, missy," Tom said.

"Now now. No need to be rude. I'm keeping the snakes from eating you." She lowered her voice. "Listen, you want to save your friends, right? You came all the way here and you asked Jaxer of all people to come help you. You can do this. You just need to focus so we can save your friends."

"Why are you being nice to him?" Jaxer asked. "He's an ass."

She shrugged. "So are you, and I'm still nice to you. Most of the time."

Tom chuckled. "Ah, I knew I liked you, missus."

"Ha! Just figure out that staff." She turned back to Jaxer. "And you get with the distractions. He'll focus better if he's not worried about that wall of snakes that's as high as his head now."

Which it was, and that was terrifying. The larger red-eyed snakes were bumping through the wall of snakes, slamming against her shield, hard enough to be terrifying. The leprechaun at the top of the four threw her head back and laughed as some of the large red snakes rose up beside her and struck at the shield simultaneously.

"You won't hold us out forever," she screamed. And the snake across her forehead slid around so that its face pointed right at Cary.

Cary took in a gulp of air, filled with the taste of churned dirt and pine and that weird dry snake scent, and made sure she was half a foot in front of Jaxer and Tom.

Then a series of fireworks started overhead.

Fireworks?

She glanced back at Jaxer. Before she could ask, a flute started playing. She couldn't see anyone with a flute. But the sound carried through the snakes, and to her amazement, some of them rose up out of the mass of other snakes, pointing in the same direction, as if they were looking for the source of the flute music, too.

More bright colored lights and sparkles exploded overhead in the tree branches. The leprechaun at the top of the stack looked up, holding a hand over her eyes as a flash of brightness exploding into a series of falling white stars.

Real fireworks would have caught the trees on fire and filled the forest with smoke. So she was glad Jaxer hadn't gone that far with his illusion. But what he was doing had made the snakes and the leprechauns shift their focus, drawing their attention away from the attack on her shield.

Tom's shoulders visibly relaxed and he brought the staff close to his face as he inspected the tip of it.

It was mostly just an ordinary long stick, like a thick wooden walking stick. But the top of it, when she looked closer, had a little red jewel embedded in the wood. She hadn't noticed that earlier. Though, to be fair, she hadn't taken a good, long look at the staff before either because…well, snakes.

"What's the ruby do?" she asked pointing to the jewel.

"That's not a ruby," Tom said. "It's called a firestone. A Faery stone. Don't see it outside Faery much."

"Why not?"

"Starts fires if yer not careful," he said with a shrug.

Cary glanced at all the trees around them. "Be careful then."

Tom's snort held a lot of meaning.

More fireworks went off overhead, and the sound of flute music increased, coming from two different directions now.

"Good illusions," Cary said to Jaxer.

"Thank you."

"Don't get too cocky," Tom said. "You've only distracted some of them."

"If you hadn't called forty thousand more, we wouldn't be in this mess."

"Boys," Cary said, raising her hands, palms facing them. "While I love the banter, we need to put a lid on it until after we get rid of scary snakes and save the leprechauns."

"Save us?" the top leprechaun said, then laughed. "We are so much more now. Save us? You should be more concerned with yerself."

"Oh, I am. Don't you worry about that. Plenty concerned for myself." She really wanted to rush Tom. She knew he'd figure this out better if she didn't, but she really wanted to rush him now.

"Alright," Tom muttered, mostly to himself. "Misinterpreting a few of these symbols here. Not great with ogham."

"There's writing?"

Cary leaned over to look at the staff. Sure enough, amidst the ordinary whorls and lumps and bumps of a polished wooden stick were black slashes and lines etched into the brown. The black slashes turned purple as she stared at them, seeming to almost come off the stick in a weirdly disorienting 3D movie effect that made her straighten and blink.

She glanced back at the red jewel. It looked like it was pulsing now, and there were sparkling white lights flickering around in the depth of the red.

"The firestone is glittering," Cary said. "You're not about to catch something on fire, are you?"

Tom looked up at the stone, then back down at the ancient writing along the staff. "Nope. Think that might be a good sign."

"Why is the writing purple and floating above the staff now?" she asked, still staring at the weird effect.

"The writing is floating for ye?" Tom asked, moving closer to her. "Tell me what you see."

"Just a lot of lines crossing over each other. I don't read ogham."

Though it was one of the ancient writings she was supposed to have learned by now. Just like runes. And she hadn't yet. Because there was just so damned much to learn. She winced a little as she glanced at Jaxer. Always more to learn and never enough time.

"They aren't floating for me," Tom said. "They're doing that for you. Tell me what you see. Exactly."

She tried her best to describe the pattern she was seeing. The lines crossing over other lines. The scattering of star patterns, diamonds with lines through them, squared curves. But mostly just lines with other lines crossing them.

"I can't read it," she repeated. "Does what I gave you help at all?"

"It does," Tom said with a quiet sigh. "It does. That's what I was missing."

"What?"

"Some of the writing is not in this realm, see. It's on the staff without being on the staff, and I couldn't see it." He frowned at her. "You must be some witch to be able to see writing linked to Faery."

"Sure. That's me." She forced a smile.

But she had no idea why she could see the floating letters. She had a feeling that had to do with her Protector magic. While it primarily just made her a walking Kevlar vest, the magic did occasionally give her the necessary skills she needed to save people. Mostly, she just had to stubbornly stand in the way. But every so often, she needed to do a little more—like sprint really fast or, apparently, read ancient writing that was in a different realm—and the Protector magic gave her those abilities.

She supposed in this case, since neither Tom nor Jaxer seemed able to see the floating letters, her Protector magic gave her that skill so they could save the day. Which was a pretty neat trick she intended on discussing with Jaxer later.

Specifically, she wanted to know why the powers allowed her to *see* the floating writing, but didn't magically give her the skill to *read* the magical writing? Why not help her read it, too?

A red-eyed snake slammed hard against her shield just then, one of the huge ones with the head the size of a basset hound, and that refocused Cary on the immediate dangers. Questions for her mentor could wait.

"Got it," Tom said again. But he sounded a lot less confident than the last time he'd said that.

And since the last time he'd said that, he'd accidentally called more snakes, his lack of confidence this time was not reassuring.

More fireworks exploded overhead and a rolling series of flute music ran manically through the trees, like Pan had gone a bit mad. The snakes were divided, some moving around the trees in pursuit of the flutes. Some were standing on their tails, looking up, apparently watching the fireworks. Others were still attacking her shield. Cary could see the bottom leprechaun on the stack again, which was something of a relief, but the wall of snakes still rose to his chest.

Everything outside her shield was pandemonium and chaos. And if they didn't do something soon, this was only going to get worse.

This time when Tom raised the staff, he held it out to one side, his free hand spread high in the air. He said something in a language Cary didn't know—which was most of them, and wasn't that embarrassing —and then he started chanting what she might have thought was a spell, but it seemed to just be the same series of words over and over.

The snakes hissed. The leprechauns howled and cursed. The giant red-eyed snakes slammed harder against her shield.

Tom raised his voice, chanting so loud, his deep voice boomed over the top of all the other noise.

And then even louder. As if he was speaking into a microphone and the sound broadcast out over the snakes via giant speakers. He almost fumbled at that sudden increase in sound, but recaptured the rhythm of the chant with only a single missed beat. He gave Jaxer a side-eyed glare. Jaxer tried to look innocent, which always failed spectacularly.

With Jaxer's magical help amplifying the chant, Tom's voice echoed through the trees. The snakes' writhing churned to frantic movement. But the wall of them started to subside. Fewer snakes piled against her shield. Fewer snakes covering the leprechaun at the bottom of the stack. The soil reappeared through the snake bodies.

"It's working," Cary said. "Keep going."

She stepped forward, forcing the remaining snakes back a bit, forcing the stack of leprechauns to move backward.

"We will not go into the sea!" the top leprechaun screamed. "We will rule!"

"Yeah, no. I don't think that's a good idea," Cary said. "But maybe just don't try to rule everyone, and then you won't have to go back to the sea."

She glanced back at Jaxer. He shrugged. "Not sure how all this works," he said. "Have to ask Tom when he's done."

Tom didn't stop chanting, which was good since the snakes were retreating, but he did give Jaxer another side-eyed look that told Cary absolutely nothing.

"No!" the leprechauns standing on each other's shoulders shouted at once. "We will not go!"

But the red-eyed, little black snakes circling their heads started to writhe more, swarming around the leprechauns' foreheads and through their hair, faster and faster. The leprechaun at the bottom of the four, blinked a few times and shook his head. The snake in his hair wove over his forehead again and the blinking stopped. But then one of the leprechauns in the middle started shaking her head. And then the top one started swatting at her ears.

The four wobbled, swaying. Shit. They were going to fall.

Cary took a single step forward before she realized she couldn't catch them without risking the protection she had on Jaxer and Tom. She glanced between the surrounding snakes, much fewer in number now, and the leprechauns. The soil was so churned up, hopefully this would be a soft landing, because the leprechaun at the top of the stack wobbled so much, the whole lot of them bent sideways.

And the whole thing came crashing down. All four tumbling into the middle of the remaining snakes and dirt. Cary winced and still took another step forward, wanting to help.

"You all okay?" she called, cringing a little.

Yes, yes, they'd technically been with the bad guys, but not voluntarily. She was still hoping they could get all the leprechauns out of this without damage. And get the red-eyed snakes sent back to… well, wherever they came from. Given the staff, that was probably the sea.

The leprechauns scrambled to their feet. Two of them reached up frantically into their hair and grabbed at the snakes. One hissed in pain and drew his hand back, the two deep punctures in the soft part of his hand obvious even at a distance.

The second leprechaun got her snake dislodged and was holding it at arm's length as it writhed and flipped out its tail toward her. Its forked tongue flickered in the air. Its red eyes glowed like light reflecting through a ruby. The leprechaun shivered and tossed the snake away, into the trees.

One of the big snakes rose up suddenly out of the soil, in the path of the little black snake, and the little black snake slammed against the larger one, then…

Just melted into the larger snake.

"Whoa." Cary blinked a few times, not sure she'd seen that right. "Did the little snake just, like, become part of the larger snake? Did I really see that?"

"You really saw that," Jaxer said.

The larger snake started toward the leprechauns.

"Oh. Not good." Cary waved at them. "Throw your black snakes at that big one and then get over here. Get behind me. Quick quick quick quick." Panic had her heartbeat hammering and her waving frantic. She took another step closer, wondering if she could physically pull them back before the large snake reached them.

Another leprechaun got his snake dislodged and tossed it, badly, toward the larger snake. Then he charged toward Cary and slid behind her like his life depended on it. Which, she had a feeling, it sort of did.

His snake slithered up to the large snake, who paused and lifted the top half of its body high, hovering in the air like it was about to strike. The smaller snake crawled up the larger one's length and once again, just…melted into the big one. Becoming a part of it. A black line across its green scales.

Cary blinked. The large one had a lot of black lines on its scales. Lots and lots of black lines.

"Shit. Do you think all those lines can become more snakes?"

"Uh," Jaxer said.

Which was a very very bad sign.

6

———

ary waved even more frantically at the leprechauns, her arms flailing ridiculously, and she found herself bouncing from one foot to the other in her desperation to hurry them to her as the large red-eyed snake with all the lines that could possibly be smaller snakes lowered slowly back to the dark, churned up soil.

The first leprechaun who'd freed herself from the black snake looked between the larger snake and Cary a few times. Then grabbed the snake from the hair of one of her compatriots and flung it at the larger snake. Her throw was better than the leprechaun already behind Cary. She smacked the larger snake right between the eyes with the black snake. The larger animal's red eyes flared bright. It stopped as the little black snake slithered over its head and down the length of its body until it melted into yet another line of scales.

A second large snake rose up out of the ground a few feet to Cary's right. She clamped her teeth together to keep from screeching at the suddenness of the second large snake's appearance. The two newly freed leprechauns raced to Cary, clambering to get behind her before the new snake reached them.

It lunged, fast enough to make Cary jump, but missed the two leprechauns by inches. When it turned toward them again, it came up against Cary's shield.

Unfortunately, now that snake was between Cary and the remaining leprechaun—who was sandwiched between two of the large snakes. And that remaining leprechaun hadn't removed her black snake from her person yet.

"Shit shit shit," Cary cursed. "Why isn't the staff getting rid of the red-eyed bastards?" This she muttered to Jaxer so she wouldn't throw Tom off.

His voice was starting to crack as he chanted louder, as his voice boomed through the pine trees, aided by Jaxer's amplification magic. The mass of snakes that had carpeted the ground were mostly gone now. Only the very large ones and a knot of littler black snakes remained.

But none of them seemed to be driven off by the chant.

And there was still one leprechaun trapped out in the middle of them all.

The trapped leprechaun turned toward Cary, her green eyes were wide and frantic, but when she spoke, it was in the same tone as she'd used when standing on her compatriots' shoulders.

"We will not be driven out. It is our time. *Our* time. We have waited long enough." She lunged forward, toward Tom, toward the staff.

Her movements were jerky and awkward, like only part of her wanted to move the way she was moving.

"I have to get that snake off her," Cary said to Jaxer.

Jaxer looked at the remaining snakes encircling their group. "If you go to her, you'll drop the shield on us," he murmured near her ear. "She's not in the right position yet."

"Can you keep everyone safe until I get back?" She looked between her charges and the struggling leprechaun. "Tom's chant should keep the snakes sort of back, right?"

Jaxer glanced around. "Okay. I've got these four. Go get her."

Jaxer rolled his hand in the air, and suddenly there were walls rising up around the large snakes. Brick walls that looked solid and thick. Hisses rose in protest, so loud, they made Cary flinch.

She didn't wait to see if the snakes could get through Jaxer's glamour—his illusions were usually so solid, they *felt* real so she hoped that worked against the snakes. She charged the remaining leprechaun, wrapped an arm around her, and snatched the snake out of her hair. The snake hissed and lunged at Cary's face. Cary squeaked and tossed the little bastard away, throwing it randomly at a tree. The snake raced toward her, but this time hit her shield and bounced backward.

Cary released a breath. She wasn't going to look at snakes in quite the same way again after this.

To the leprechaun, she said, "Sorry about this." Then she picked her up and ran back to Jaxer and the others.

Protector magic gave her both the strength to carry an adult leprechaun and the speed to reach the others before any of the larger snakes broke through Jaxer's wall illusions.

But only just.

The shattering of bricks made her duck even though she knew she was safe because she was protecting everyone else. And also because the bricks were just an illusion Jaxer had created. But glamour was Jaxer's strongest magic, and he could make his illusions feel and seem so real, she wouldn't be surprised if getting beaned by one of those imaginary bricks actually did hurt.

"Everyone okay?" Cary asked, holding the final leprechaun until she got her feet under and stood steadily.

Tom stopped chanting, the sudden silence filling the trees as loudly as the sound had.

Cary spun to face him. He'd lowered his arms. The staff to his side. As he stared up.

She finished her turn to see five large red-eyed snakes hovering above them, standing high on their tails so that their heads hung directly over Cary and her charges.

"Uhm?" She pushed all of the leprechauns behind her and made sure she was between the snakes and Tom and Jaxer. "So… What's happening now?"

"Missing something in the staff," Tom murmured. "Can't get rid of these bastards. The others are all gone. They can't call the ordinary snakes back now, not for a bit. But… I can't make them go away."

"I'm open to ideas here," Cary said, staring up at the snakes, their red-eyes looking larger and brighter and much too close.

A sort of falling sensation made her jerk. She blinked a few times and looked away.

"Yeah, I wouldn't look at them in the eyes," Jaxer said. "You'll be fine, but it might get a little disorienting."

"Ya think," she said, shaking her head hard. "Could have warned me about that."

"Your…shield's working. You're fine. But their efforts might give you a headache even if they can't get through to you."

"Lovely." She glanced at the leprechauns. "Any thoughts on what we should do now?"

"Aster needs a healer," the first leprechaun to free herself said. She had her arms around the leprechaun who'd been bitten. He was shivering and holding his hand, sweat beading on his brow and matting his brown hair to his neck.

"Shit. Venom. They do venom. That's…bad." She didn't have any convenient anti-venom for magic snakes on her. And she wasn't a healer. There was a lot her Protector magic, including healing *her* faster than a normal human woman would heal. But she couldn't heal other people's injuries.

She gave Jaxer a frantic look.

He faced the big spruce tree behind them. Then scanned the other trees. And finally nodded. "I can get them into Faery, to a healer. But that'll mean leaving you and Tom behind." He scowled at Tom. "I don't trust him."

"Don't have to. I just need him around to keep…everyone safe. You get the others out of here. Tom and I will, hopefully, figure out the snakes."

"Get them out," Tom said, his gaze still on the large creatures hovering over them. "We'll be fine."

Jaxer took the other side of the sick leprechaun, and the five of them moved to a tree that was still inside Cary's protection—behind her but not too far, and with Cary standing between the tree and the snakes. She watched as Jaxer moved everyone around the base of the tree, circling once, and then…

Just at the base of a tree, a section of the ground opened up, like a set of stairs going into the earth. Jaxer ushered the four leprechauns down the stairs ahead of him.

From the top of the stairs, Jaxer met her gaze. "I'll be back as soon as I get them to a healer. Don't trust that leprechaun."

She nodded but waved at him to hurry him up. The sick leprechaun didn't have time for last minute warnings. Who knew how fast venom from red-eyed snakes moved through leprechaun blood?

Jaxer gave her a long look. Scowled at Tom.

Then disappeared down the stairs.

7

The ground sealed over Jaxer as if there had never been an opening and a stairway leading down into the earth.

"Faery is weird," Cary said, mostly to herself.

"Surely it is. Now, what else can you do besides shielding and seeing ogham runes?"

She noticed he said "seeing" rather than "reading" but couldn't be offended since that was very accurate. "Depends on the situation," she hedged.

She really couldn't *do* anything much. What needed to be done, yes. But mostly what *needed* to be done was her to just stand in between bad guys and good guys until the bad guys got bored and went home.

"What can you do?" she asked. "You have the staff. You drove away the other snakes. What's going on with these red-eyed bastards?"

"We are not so easily led," one of the red-eyed snakes hissed.

Ah. So. They spoke. And not just through the captured and manipulated leprechauns. That was…creepy.

The five large red-eyed snakes leaned down closer, all at the same time. Cary couldn't tell if they were trying to get through her shield or just leaning closer to look at them better. Or maybe they had to be that close to make themselves heard? Or maybe they were just trying to scare them.

If the last, it was working.

The snakes were very large and their red eyes glowed like illuminated rubies and while she could stand here and keep her and Tom safe all day, she would rather not have the large snakes unleash all those little black snakes that covered their scales looking like black lines. Since the little bastards were both dangerous for usurping a person's will and also venomous.

She thought about how she'd snatched the black snake off the last leprechaun's head and tossed it away. The memory made her shiver, hard. She was probably safe from getting bitten. And she'd heal from venom even if she got bitten because she'd need to in order to keep protecting her vulnerable charge. Protector magic was convenient that way. But the fact that she'd been that close to a venomous bite wasn't a pleasant memory.

This was why she'd restricted her snake experience to constrictors. Their bite hurt, but at least it wasn't a toxic killing machine. And yes, yes, *constricting*. But you could avoid getting choked by a snake if you were careful. Mostly.

She shook off the mental ramblings as the five snakes leaned down even farther and the one who'd spoken flicked out its tongue.

"Your magic tastes of Faery," it hissed.

"Not sure why," she said. She knew exactly why. "Maybe you're tasting the leprechaun."

"I'd rather not be tasted by one of these red-eyed bastards," Tom said.

"Can't really blame you. Any progress on driving them off?"

"Can't see the writing you saw," he said. "Want to read me some of the other runes?"

"Sure."

She turned sideways to the snakes while still keeping Tom safely behind her. And that took an act of will because one of the large snakes made a diving strike at them, which resulted in its nose getting smashed against her shield.

But the sudden strike still made her jump. Which was just embarrassing in front of Tom.

"Hold it up," she motioned for him to raise the old monk's staff. Or maybe it was Faery's staff? She'd have to work that out later. She stared at the smoothed wood, first glancing at the imbedded firestone in the top of the staff, then let her gaze move over the rest of the length, down to the blackened lines cut into the wood. They rose up again, purple 3D images rising into the air above the staff.

"That is so weird," she murmured. She frowned at them. "I'm pretty sure I told you what all of these were already. I'll tell you again." Since she couldn't read them, it was another series of, "This one is a line with three lines coming off it at a downward angle. And this one is another line with four lines cut across it. And this one is a diamond with a line through the middle. And…" Until she'd told him what all the runes she could see were. He had to do the interpreting of the symbols. But at least one of them could read ogham.

When she was finished, Tom cursed. Colorfully and with a lot of feeling. "Buggering fuckbastards," he the rant. "There's nothing we missed. Nothing there to tell me how to get rid of the red-eyed arseholes."

"You cannot get rid of us," the talking snake hissed. "We will break through your barrier and retrieve the staff. We will rule!"

Cary tried to ignore the hissing snake since its voice was like nails on a chalkboard, and instead kept her attention on the staff—bad guys always issued a ton of similar threats when they couldn't get past her shield anyway. She wasn't hearing anything particularly new or interesting from this bad guy.

Her gaze stopped once again on the firestone at the top of the staff. "You suppose that might do something…useful. In this situation? Like, it's probably not there just for decoration, right?"

Tom scowled at the firestone, shaking the staff a little as if that would make the answers fall out of it. "Could be. But we just hid this thing. We weren't told how it all worked."

"Why were leprechauns put in charge of hiding the staff? And why out of Faery?"

"Out of Faery because it's too dangerous to keep this thing in Faery now." He nodded at the snakes. "They might be able to follow it there."

She opened her mouth to ask more questions but snapped it shut a beat later so she didn't derail Tom's explanation. She was mostly interested why the leprechauns had been put in charge of the thing.

"Us," Tom said with a little shrug. "Because aren't we good at hiding things at the ends of rainbows."

She snorted. Then gave him a closer look. "That's a myth. The pot of gold at the end of the rainbow nonsense. And the rainbow was just that gold-triggered passage thingy you did to get us here. Right? That's what you and Jaxer *just* told me. Were you lying?"

Tom grinned. "Sure and don't we always. Never trust a leprechaun, Cary. They're sneaky bastards."

"Ha!" But also, "Thanks for the answers. I guess. So... The firestone. How might that help in this particular situation, do you think?"

Tom glared at the stone. "Hell if I know. No one saw fit to give us a primer on the thing."

"Probably because you're sneaky bastards," she said.

"True. Still, could use that bit of knowledge about now, right."

Cary tilted her head to one side as she stared at the stone. One of the huge snakes lunged at them and came up hard against her shield. She didn't glance up, but Tom did and his eyebrows rose.

"Some shield," he commented.

"It's a pretty good one," she said, her attention on the staff. "Can I hold it a second?" She made a face. "I won't accidentally unleash a bunch of snakes like you did, if I just hold it?"

Tom gave her a little snarl at the reminder he'd made the snake situation worse before making it better. But he handed her the staff. "Just don't go shaking it about. Leave that to the expert."

She snorted. "Expert. Right." She held the long, smooth length of wood with two hands and brought the top of it closer to her face so she could get a better angle on the firestone.

Three of the five snakes dove at her shield. She ignored them. But the sounds of them bouncing off the barrier were a little distracting. She couldn't feel the hits. She didn't even feel the shield. She just had to trust it was there. But she could hear the huge snakes pinging off the solid dome of her Protector magic. Lot of loud thumps.

She turned the firestone a little more, angling it so it caught the sun.

And blinked a few times. Then looked closer. "Here." She waved Tom closer. "You seeing this?"

The stone winked and glowed just like the snakes' red eyes. Bright and almost the identical color. But what was even more interesting were the wiggling lines inside the stone. Black lines. Not like the ogham runes, but like…

"Looks like the little black snakes that melted back into the bigger bastards' scales," Tom muttered.

"Ew. You think there are snakes inside the stone?"

"Possible. Wouldn't be the first stone in the history of this realm or mine to hold something more than minerals and magic."

"Great. So if I'm not careful, I might unleash more red-eyed snakes?"

"Or ye could capture them with the stone, draw them into it." Tom's green eyes narrowed as he stared at the thing.

"How, exactly, would I do that? Or you do that. You. Since you're our resident staff wielder here."

"Anyone holding it can wield it, Cary. And you're holding it."

"You just don't want to get blamed for unleashing a snake plague if that's what the firestone does."

"True," he said without any regret or shame. "But I think ye may be on to something. With the stone there being the key."

"No!" hissed the talking snake. "We will not go back into the sea."

While Cary could hear the ocean not that far away, none of the other snakes had been forced into the sea. They'd just been sent away.

"They didn't get sent into the sea, did they? The other snakes?" Just to confirm.

"No. Just back to where they came from. Broke the sway these had on them."

She looked up at the talking snake. It lunged down at her, an abrupt strike that might have made her jump if she wasn't expecting it this time. The other four also lunged at her shield, to no avail. She liked that word. Avail. Good word.

"Are you talking about the actual sea? The actual ocean? Or is that a metaphor?" she asked the talking snake. She wasn't really expecting an answer.

And she wasn't disappointed. "We will not go back. We will drive your kind into the sea where you belong!"

She looked at the firestone again. "This thing generally catches stuff on fire, right? That's why it's called a firestone. But there are also these snake-like thingies writhing away in here." She shivered. "So maybe… Maybe this is the sea in the metaphor?"

"Sea of fire?" Tom asked.

"I mean…people do use that phrase about things. Like lava and stuff. Not unheard of. Sea of fire. Something that could get lost in translation over the centuries. Until all that anyone remembers is sea." Mostly to herself, she murmured, "Like pots of gold and the end of rainbows."

She waved the staff back and forth in front of her, and sure enough, the interior of the firestone looked to rock and roll like there was liquid inside the crystalline shell.

"Cool," she murmured. Then, "Well, maybe in this case, hot."

She held the staff up. "If I fuck this up and unleash more snakes, I'm going to tell Jaxer it was your fault," she told Tom without any shame.

"He'd find a way to blame me even if you did come clean."

"There's a story there," she said.

"For a later time and a larger pint," he said.

"Deal." She gestured Tom to get farther behind her. "You had to chant, because just waving the thing around didn't help. You think you could repeat that chant while I'm holding the staff?"

"What makes ye think you'll get a better response than I did? That there little stone didn't do a thing for me."

She had no idea what made her think this would work. She was just sort of hoping her Protector magic would give her what she needed to make it work. She'd never tried anything like this. But what the hell? Couldn't hurt.

Or, well, it could because she could unleash a plague of snakes. But Tom knew how to put those back now.

"Just do your chant," she said. "I'm going to do…" She frowned a little. Glanced at the lines on the large snakes, thought of the way the smaller snakes had just…merged with the large snake and become a part of it…

"What if I… What if I touch the snakes with the stone?" She didn't want to literally unleash a sea of fire onto the Oregon coast because that would be bad. But if the snakes got sucked back *into* the sea of fire inside the stone… "That could work, right?"

"They'll kill you the minute you get within striking distance," Tom said matter-of-factly. "Or they'll unleash all them little black bastards to take over yer mind. Wouldn't recommend that course of action at all at all."

"Any better ideas?"

"Not a one."

"Then we'll try this. Worst that could happen…"

Well, some really bad things could happen, so she decided not to tempt fate by listing the possibilities out loud.

Something about tempting Murphy's Law on St. Patrick's Day while she was standing in the woods with a leprechaun trying to drive out snakes seemed like a really bad idea.

"You're a bit mad," Tom said. "I like that about you."

"Thanks. Now stay behind me. That'll help both of us." She didn't explain how. "And do that chanting thing, whatever it was."

"Good luck," Tom said.

And they started toward the talking snake.

8

"We will not go back!" Talking Snake roared, so loud it reverberated around the pines, bouncing around the woods in a shattering echo at odds with the beautiful bright, cold spring day.

Cary moved closer, holding the staff in front of her like a shield as Tom started to chant.

"No!" The snake dropped lower, putting its eyes level with hers.

And she felt that swing of vertigo, that disorientation that made her want to stumble. Worse than fucking vampire stares. At least she could meet a vampire's gaze without any effect while she was protecting someone. Why the hell didn't that work on the snakes?

She realized it probably was since she wasn't being mesmerized by the giant beastie. But the vertigo was not a pleasant sensation. She avoided the snake's eyes, looking at its snout and flicking tongue instead. That forked tongue tasted the air before the snake reared back so it was swaying several feet over her head.

All five snakes lunged at her at the same time then. Sharp fangs she hadn't paid much attention to before dropping against her shield with a clank, and the sound of their scales over the churned-up soil was more metal-against-metal sounding than it should have been.

151

She hadn't gotten close enough to feel any of the large snakes' scales. The small black one had felt like normal snake skin. Dry and smooth and a little lumpy. But that sound of metal moving against metal made her wonder if the larger snakes had armored scales.

And wouldn't that just be typical.

She pushed forward, pointed the staff in front of her, using its length to keep some distance between herself and the talking snake. Her shield kept the other snakes from getting at her and Tom, pushing them back. But where normally her shield would have shoved Talking Snake backward too, this time she was able to get closer to it.

Close enough she thumped it with the firestone end of the staff, right in the center of its raised body.

Tom continued to chant, but for a long moment, nothing happened.

The snake hissed a sound like a laugh. Cary had a moment to curse and wonder what else she needed to do to get these assholes inside the firestone—or if that was even an option. She'd been guessing, and it seemed like her guesses were wrong.

Then, suddenly, the little black snakes started reappearing where the lines of black scales had marked their location along the length of the larger snake's body. Not just one or two, but hundreds of them popped up out of Talking Snake's scales.

"Fuck. I think I've messed up," she said.

Tom didn't stop chanting to berate her, but she could feel his fist clenching her leather jacket.

She opened her mouth to ask for suggestions, then snapped it shut as the little black snakes rushed toward the staff. It took an act of will —and her instinctive "freeze in place" response to threat—to keep her from jerking backward and moving the staff off the larger snake. That reaction proved perfect.

Because all those little black snakes went streaming *into* the firestone.

Hundreds of them flowed from the larger snake's body into the firestone. As they went, the larger snake grew smaller, and smaller. She had to keep lowering the staff to keep it in contact with Talking Snake.

Talking Snake screeched a sound that reminded Cary of pretend dinosaur noises from movies, even as it shrank. The other four snakes started to screech as well. And when she looked, she could see hundreds of little red-eyed black snakes streaming from them as well.

All of those littler snakes raced into the firestone, and with each wave of snakes vanishing into the red gem, the stone pulsed brighter. Cary could feel the heat from it now, too. No ordinary cold bit of crystal. The heat pumped from the stone, like a miniature sun, growing and glowing.

The shrieking grew so loud, she wanted to cover her ears. But she kept the end of the staff pressed against the ever shrinking Talking Snake. Tom continued to chant.

And more and more black snakes raced into the stone at the tip of the staff.

She wasn't sure how much time passed, minutes at most, but almost as suddenly as it had started, the black snakes stopped streaming into the stone.

All that remained were five small green snakes with deep red eyes. She still had the staff against one of the smaller snakes. It continued to screech. But now the sounds were squeaky like a child's toy. Nothing that shook the ground.

And then the five green snakes slithered into the stone, reluctantly, with jerky, abrupt, jumping movements.

Still, in they went. Until the pointed tail of the very last one disappeared into the stone.

A flash of bright red light filled the clearing, the heat strong enough to steal Cary's breath. Sweat streamed down her back.

She closed her eyes against the glare and counted to five.

When the bright glow behind her closed lids eased, Cary blinked her eyes open again.

The trees were lit by ordinary sunshine. A cold breeze brushed against her sweaty temples. The scents of pine needles and churned dirt traveled on that breeze. But no more of the musty dry snake smell.

Just a very faint scent of burnt sap.

She didn't want to think too close about that burnt sap smell.

"Did we do it?" Tom asked, his hold on her jacket easing.

She straightened, set the bottom of the staff against the ground, and looked into the firestone. It continued to roll like there was liquid inside. There were still a bunch of wiggling black lines inside. Didn't look to be more than there'd been before. But she couldn't be certain of that.

"I think we did it," she said. She looked around. No snakes. No fire or lava setting the coast on fire. Nothing. Just churned up soil and pine trees. "I think we did it."

"Well done!" Tom thumped her on the back, hard enough to make her stumble forward a step.

She rolled her eyes at him, but also grinned because… Well, they'd done it!

"Well now. And wasn't that an adventure." Tom straightened his beautifully cut cuffs and snapped down his vest beneath the suit jacket. "Not saying I'd like to do that every day, mind. But think it's deserving of a pint. You in?"

"I could do with a pint," she said.

Just as a hole in the ground opened up.

And Jaxer walked out.

"What happened?" She hurried to him. "Are the others safe? Is… Aster, right? Is Aster okay?"

Jaxer looked around the trees. "Where are the snakes? What happened?"

"You first. Aster?"

"With a healer and doing well. They'll get the venom out of him. They said Aster should have a complete recovery. The others are being looked at to, and the healer is ensuring there was no permanent damage from the snake mesmerism."

Cary's shoulders sagged in relief.

"Now what the hell happened to the snakes?"

Cary, with a few of the details filled in by Tom, caught Jaxer up on the whereabouts of the snakes.

He stared at the firestone in the staff after they'd finished. "Huh." Was his only response.

"That's all I get for figuring this out?" she pouted. "A huh?"

"Would you prefer a 'well done'?"

"Well, yeah. I mean the only reason I'm here is because of you. A little appreciation would be nice."

Jaxer grinned and kissed her on the cheek. "Good job," he said. "Well done."

She scowled at the kiss, but preened at his approval. It was a little embarrassing that she wanted his approval. But he was her mentor, and it felt good when he acknowledged that she'd done well. She'd been very out of her depth when she'd been tricked into this job. The fact that she could do it now seemed like a pretty impressive accomplishment to her.

She imagined it would feel even better if her *bosses* would acknowledge that. But Wisat and Liruk were harder to please. Especially Liruk.

"What about that pint?" Tom said. "Think we've all earned it."

Jaxer gave Tom a look, but didn't argue about the beer.

"What do we do with the staff?" Cary asked. She'd been holding it this whole time and was a little reluctant to just set it down after what had crawled into it. She didn't want to accidentally let all those red-eyed assholes back out again.

"Ah, now, that I can take care of for you." Tom held his hand out for the staff.

Jaxer let out a long breath, his frown creasing his normally smooth brow. Cary hesitated at that look, but when he gave her a slight nod, she handed the staff back to Tom.

Tom proceeded to hunt around the giant spruce tree for a little bit. Then he set the staff against the bark. The staff faded into the tree, blending in with it until Cary could no longer see it amidst the straight lines of bark. Not even the red firestone marked the location of the staff anymore.

She crossed the tree and touched the spot where the staff had disappeared. Couldn't feel it. The area just felt like the rest of the rough bark. She even came away with a little sap on her hand.

She rubbed the sticky stuff between her fingers absently as she stared at the spot where the staff was supposed to be. "That's a very cool trick," she said. "No one can find it?"

"Not if they don't know the way to the end of the rainbow," Tom said with a smirk.

She huffed out a half laugh. Jaxer snorted. Tom grinned.

"You are such an ass," Jaxer said.

"And wouldn't you know exactly what that takes," Tom returned. "Being as how you're such a giant one, yerself."

"Okay, let's go get that beer now," Cary interrupted. "Before the two of you come to blows. And maybe if you get drunk enough, you'll tell me what started all the animosity."

"It was his fault," Jaxer said.

"Well and if that isn't the pot calling the kettle black," Tom returned. "Most would say the start of all this was down to you."

Cary raised a hand. "Beer first. Delightfully interesting story second."

"No green beer," Tom and Jaxer said at the same time.

She grinned when they scowled at each other. "No green beer," she agreed. "Now, open up that rainbow passage and get us back to the city. I know the perfect place."

"Should we be scared?" Tom asked Jaxer as he did a thing with his hands that opened a portal circled in a rainbow of colored lights.

"Yes," Jaxer said with a vicious grin.

Cary chuckled and followed the faery and the leprechaun back down the rainbow.

Weirdest St. Patrick's Day ever.

CARY'S BELTANE NIGHT OUT

Beltane, bonfires, magic…and human sacrifice?

When Cary Redmond ends up at a Beltane celebration with her best friend, the witch Angie Jordan, Cary knows she's in for an interesting night. Trouble swirls in the air right alongside the campfire smell. Magic and danger and people to protect. All in a night's work for a magical Protector and her powerful best friend. But Cary gets a lot more than she bargains for.

A field full of bespelled pagans trying to throw themselves into a giant bonfire only starts a night of deadly danger. Because inside that fire, the real threat lurks. A threat impossible to destroy.

And if Cary can't figure out what's going on in time, a lot of people will burn.

1

The heat from the pickup-truck-sized bonfire washed across Cary's front while cold air chilled her back. The contrast made her shiver. And if she weren't so confused about why she was at this Beltane celebration, she might have enjoyed the heat.

The surrounding field was huge and filled with maybe fifty neopagans, Wiccans, and probably a few magic-wielding witches as well. All of then standing around the large bonfire, hands in the air, humming something Cary couldn't catch. The night was dark and moonless. And since they were in the middle of nothing much more than vineyards about half way between Portland and Eugene, the black sky was blanketed with stars.

Again, something she might have enjoyed if she'd been here for any expected and straightforward reason. Especially since she was here with one of her best friends who was an amateur astronomer.

And, also, one of the magic-wielding witches.

"So, you haven't been to this Beltane celebration before?" Cary asked, leaning close to Angie so she could whisper and still be heard over the group hum.

"Nope." Angie nodded, her gaze straight ahead.

"You're a solitary witch who doesn't go in for group activities. Right?"

"Right."

"That hasn't changed?"

"Nope."

"And you're not looking for any fertility help?"

That drew a harsh glare from Angie. "Hell no. If I haven't wanted kids before—ever—what makes you think I would suddenly change my mind now?"

"I don't know." Cary shrugged. "Ghost possession? Evil spell?"

Angie's mouth twitched and her expression softened. In the flaring orange-red light, her green eyes sparkled. She had her shoulder length wavy brown hair pulled back in a messy bun, and was dressed in her day-off attire, which tonight involved jeans, a blue t-shirt, and light green corduroy jacket that worked well for the early May weather. If she'd been working, Angie would have worn tinkling jewelry, a poet blouse, and flowing pagan skirts with lots of moons and stars embroidered onto natural fibers.

Which was how Cary knew this had nothing to do with Angie's job. She just couldn't figure out what it *did* have to do with.

"No possession or evil spells involved," Angie said. "Definitely not looking for a fertility blessing. Ensured I didn't have to worry about any of that at twenty-nine when I finally found a doctor who'd tie my tubes."

Cary frowned a little. "Finally?"

"You would not believe how many doctors refused because 'I might change my mind,' or worse, some unspecified man in my future might want to use my uterus to reproduce."

"Ew."

"Mm hmm. Finally found a brilliant witch gynecologist who understood that I knew my own mind."

"This is a conversation we will dive deeper into at our earliest convenience," Cary said. "But in the meantime, if you're not here for fertility stuff, and you don't usually celebrate these holidays with other witches, and you brought my non-practicing Presbyterian ass here, I feel I must finally ask, *why* are we here?"

When Angie called and said she needed Cary to come with her to a field in the middle of nowhere half way between Portland and Eugene that very night, Cary had grabbed her leather jacket and keys, no questions asked. On the drive down, Angie had said she'd explain when they got where they were going. So Cary had watched the dark fields and trees beside the highway pass and waited to arrive. She hadn't really paid attention to the date. Until they'd pulled up beside a bunch of parked cars in the empty field and seen the roaring bonfire, it hadn't occurred to her it was the first of May.

And realizing it was Beltane as they'd pulled up to a Beltane celebration hadn't done anything to enlighten Cary as to the whys of their presence.

Angie let out a long breath, her gaze returning to the fire, her brow creased with her frown. The orange light cast deep shadows across her pale skin. "Honestly, I'm not entirely sure. I did a reading with a younger woman last week, a cute little pagan who planned to come to this celebration. That had nothing to do with her reading. She just mentioned it in passing. After the reading, we shook hands as she left, and I got a vision that… I'm not entirely sure what to think."

Angie was a psychic and who got glimpses at futures, and sometimes presents and pasts, when she touched things and people. She used her skills to do psychic readings for private clients, but Cary knew she was usually pretty careful about what and how much she let in during those sessions. For her own sake and for her clients' privacy.

"I've been worrying about what I saw for a week and finally thought I'd better come out here, just to make sure everything went okay."

"And brought me in case it didn't." Cary nodded.

As a magical Protector, it was her job—literally; she even got paid for it—to get between good guys and bad guys and keep the good guys safe. Her bosses, the North American Fae who created Protectors, got visions and premonition and used those to send Protectors into trouble to save the day. It wasn't a perfect system or nothing bad would ever happen. And there were only so many Protectors in the world. But they helped. Which was why Cary didn't complain about being tricked into the job. Too often.

"I'm not sure we'll be needed," Angie said. "But the image from the vision… No, it was more the feeling I got from the vision, has had me restless and worried all week. Decided I didn't want to ignore that instinct."

"Wise. Glad I can be here to help."

"Even if nothing happens?" Angie gave her a sideways look, brows raised.

"Especially if nothing happens. Never gonna complain about 'nothing bad happened' nights out."

Angie smiled crookedly. "Thanks."

They faced the fire again. From their place at the very back of the small crowd, they still had a great view of the fire as some of the flames danced higher into the sky, sending out little bright sparks. Fortunately, it had been a pretty wet spring so far, so the chances of a bush fire were low, but Cary still watched those sparks warily.

The hum from the surrounding group got a little louder. "Any idea what they're saying?" she asked Angie, still keeping her voice low.

Angie shrugged. "Hard to tell. More humming a few notes than saying words."

"Possibly relevant notes?" Magic sometimes took the form of tones and musical notes more than words, but Cary hadn't encountered that much so she couldn't be sure.

"Maybe." Angie rubbed her hands up and down her arms as a cool breeze danced through the field.

Typically for early May, the weather was a little unpredictable. Could be lovely spring warm or soggy spring cold. Sometimes in the same day. Tonight was dry, but the wind was cold and biting when it kicked up. Cary was grateful for her magical leather jacket. The magic part involved pockets that hid things if she needed to hide things and kept her keys and wallet from falling out—when your job often involved diving around to get between good guys and disaster, losing your keys was a real issue. Tonight, though, she was more grateful for the inner lining that kept the chilly breeze at bay.

The sparks from the bonfire danced higher with every swipe of wind, carrying the little bright scattering of light up over the crowd. The higher the sparks got, the more intense the humming grew.

"Are they gonna strip and dance naked around the fire?" Cary asked. "Cause the bonfire is hot but that breeze is cold and it's too damned cold out here to be naked."

Angie's lips twitched again. "They might get naked eventually. But I gotta agree, it's too cold for that shit."

Cary pulled her jacket tighter around her. It was a weird sensation though because she was actually sweating a little from the heat blast to her face. But the cold along her back made her shiver. If they'd been there just for fun, and if she'd had a little wine to drink at this stage, all this might be more entertaining.

As it was, her gut churned a little with unspecified anxiety, which was not helped by the rising sparks and increasing hum.

"Can you tell me what you saw or felt in the vision?" she asked Angie, keeping her gaze on the fire and the crowd.

"I saw someone dancing *inside* the fire. They were all flames, burning, but still dancing."

"Creepy,"

"The really creepy part was the laughter in the background as the person inside the fire charred and roasted."

"Ew. Big time ew."

"Yeah." Angie glanced around the clearing. "Future stuff can be symbolic more than literal. The vision doesn't have to represent someone actually burning in the bonfire. Especially since dancing as long as they danced in the vision would be impossible. But the whole thing was really disturbing. Like a waking nightmare. And it *felt* dangerous. Ominous."

"If it was symbolic, does that just mean someone here might be in trouble and the whole fire thing just represented the night?"

Angie shrugged. "Got me. That's the problem with future visions.

Only really know what they mean in hindsight. I prefer info on current or past happenings. Easier to work with."

Cary nodded. She wasn't even a little psychic. In fact, except for the magic her bosses gave her to channel, she was as mundane as mundane came. But she'd read and studied enough to understand Angie's predicament. Future visions were notoriously difficult. She was always amazed her bosses got so much right in theirs.

The fire climbed higher, as if they'd added fuel to it, though Cary didn't notice anyone feeding more wood into the flames. She didn't see any additional source of fuel for the fire either. And still the fire seemed to get bigger.

"Do you see your client around here?"

Angie frowned. "Not yet. She's probably on the other side of the fire."

"Should we walk around and try to find her? Or is it better if she doesn't see you?"

Angie's frown deepened. "She probably wouldn't be suspicious if she did see me but… Maybe we stay here for now."

"Whatever works."

The humming song was loud enough now, it was clear there were no words involved. Just a musical tune being offered to the flames. And every time the notes hit a certain combination, the flames rose.

That was weird. And probably significant.

She leaned into Angie. "Notice how the flames—"

"Jump with that one part of the song? Yup."

"Significant?"

"Significant."

"What's happening?"

"Got me. But it's a good question."

The bonfire was so big now, the people closest to it were dangerously near the flames. A tingling of anxiety crawled over Cary's back. And her Protector instincts started nagging her.

"Uh, yeah, something Not Good is happening or going to happen," she said. "Protector instincts are tingling."

"To get between everyone and the fire?"

Cary frowned, concentrating on what her instincts were urging her to do. She'd have assumed getting between everyone and the fire would be the goal, too. But…

"Weird." She searched the crowd. "I need to…" She didn't finish, just started around the fire, following where the crawling tension of worry led.

Angie followed without a word, placing herself carefully behind Cary.

That was how Cary's powers worked. She had to be protecting someone for the magic to happen. She had no control over it. It just… happened. And when it happened both she and her charges were safe. If she wasn't protecting anyone, she was as vulnerable to injury and death as the next person. But if she was between someone and danger, everyone was safe.

Her friends had all learned to get behind her in dangerous situations because it kept them all protected.

Angie was a super powerful witch. But her type of spellcasting took time—saying spells and setting them wasn't an instantaneous process. So when Cary and Angie worked together, Cary was able to give Angie the time she needed to cast good spells without having to also worry about not getting dead. It was a good arrangement. Especially since Cary couldn't do anything offensive in these situations. Stand between danger and good guys till the end of days? Check. Get the bad guys to go away? Not so much. Angie was a lot better at that part.

Cary's instincts led her halfway around the fire. To a young man whose eyes were closed as he swayed to the humming around him. A white man, maybe in his early-twenties, wearing nothing but a pair of pale linen pants, his short brown hair fluttering in the air currents from the flames. He was the only one in his immediate vicinity not singing the wordless tune.

She watched in growing horror as he stepped so close to the flames he was practically stepping on the edge of the bonfire. The image Angie described rose in her mind's eye, and without hesitating, Cary charged forward.

Getting between the young man and the flames was something that, if she'd thought about it at all, she would have balked. Fortunately, she'd been doing this long enough, she didn't think. The thinking only happened after the fact.

When she realized she was standing *inside* the bonfire.

2

The bonfire flames parted around Cary, but the heat at her back was intense. She wrapped her arms around the young man and gave him a shove. While the fire wasn't actually touching her—because she was now officially protecting someone from it—standing there seeing the flames on either side of her head, surrounding her in a tight u-shape, was disconcerting. Not the place any person in their right mind *wants* to stand.

She thought she smelled burning hair and had to suppress a yelp as she shoved the young man harder. She knew intellectually nothing was burning. Still. Flames everywhere. Something *should* be burning.

The young man resisted her efforts to push him away from the bonfire, and even tried to get around her.

Well fuck. That wasn't good. If her charge didn't let her protect them, if they dodged around her, the magic stopped working. And while normally she'd be bothered by that because her charge might die, in that moment while she was still standing *inside* the bonfire, she was as worried about herself as she was the young man.

"Nope. No." She heaved forward, trying to take the man with her, to get them both away from the danger zone.

He was about her same five-foot-nine height and wiry with muscle.

She'd have had a tough time pushing him around under different circumstances, because she wasn't wiry with muscle even a little bit. And to make matters worse, he was shirtless and slick with sweat. Her grip kept slipping and sliding on his arms.

But Protector magic gave her what she needed to keep someone safe. Speed to get to them on time. An immovable stance so she couldn't be shoved aside by the bad guys. And strength far outstripping her everyday physical abilities.

The young man reached around her shoulder toward the fire. "So warm," he murmured.

"Yup, warm. Lovely stuff. From a safe hundred yards away. Here we go."

While he strained toward the heat, he wasn't exactly fighting her hard. He was just really resistant to being moved out of the flames. By the time Cary had him far enough away they were no longer surrounded by fire, she was practically carrying him.

Angie stepped up close again, giving Cary another person to protect, but this time she put her back to Cary's, facing outward.

The position made Cary finally look up and around.

To see they were surrounded by the rest of the group.

Oh boy.

Cary kept her arms around the young man and stared out at the crowd. No one was humming anymore. Which might have been good if the utter silence wasn't so eerie.

The bonfire crackled behind her, its heat washing across her shoulders. They were still standing too close to those flames for her comfort. And the young man was still reaching over her shoulders toward the fire. But he wasn't exactly fighting to get back. It was more like he was stretching out to warm his hands. The night was cool enough, the wind blowing through the open field cold. But Cary wasn't taking chances the guy just needed to warm up.

Not after he'd been so intent on walking *into* the flames.

"They moved in the second you stopped him," Angie murmured, leaning close but not quite touching Cary's back. "But they didn't try attacking me."

"They look like they're in a trance to you, or is that just me?"

"Not just you."

"Got a handy spell for that?"

"Depends on if I can figure out what they were doing, what kind of trance they're in, and who's responsible."

"Wouldn't mind getting to the bottom of the who, too," Cary said, wincing a little at her phrasing. "This is magic?"

"Yup."

Which meant either it was a collective malice, or there was someone around here manipulating all these people. But who and to what end?

And what if this was a group effort? What if all fifty of these people had come all the way out here to do this? Not for a Beltane celebration but to sacrifice someone to the fire. That would be bad. And gross.

And still begged the question, why?

So she asked the question. "Would anyone like to explain what's happening and why it's happening?" She wasn't really expecting an answer. She rarely got one when she was this blunt.

So she was a little surprised when a woman stepped away from the otherwise comatose-looking crowd and said, "A sacrifice is required on this sacred night. It has been ordained. The goddess wishes it. And she will protect us throughout the year in return."

Okay. Well. There was a lot there.

The woman was a bit older than the other people in the crowd. Old enough to have gray threading handsomely through her dark brown hair and a few laugh lines around her mouth. Her pale complexion was softened by the firelight, a handy filter that made her age hard to pinpoint. But her straight baring marked a confidence with her place in the world. She was dressed in a flowing skirt and loose poet blouse— exactly the sort of outfit Angie would wear for work—and her bejeweled bare feet gave Cary the shivers. It was too cold for bare anything out here. Even with the roaring fire behind her.

She glanced around the crowd, looked at Angie. Then faced the woman again.

"Goddess?" she asked both the woman and Angie.

Cary thought that part might be an exaggeration. But in her world, she couldn't actually make that assumption. Might well be a real goddess around here. Which would probably be bad if the goddess was into burnt sacrifice.

"The goddess of all," the woman said. "She who will save and protect us."

"Sure sure. Is she, uhm, around here anywhere? Free for a chat maybe?"

"She will join us soon," the woman said.

"Oh good." Cary wasn't entirely sure that was a good thing. But it would cut to the chase. The man in her arms tugged toward the fire again, and she had to tighten her grip on him. "Hold on there, fella, we've got some things to talk about before you go walking through flames."

"I can do it," he said. "It's so warm. She'll protect me."

"The goddess?"

"Yes. She loves me."

"This isn't quite the Beltane celebration I might have expected," Cary said to no one in particular. To Angie, she said, "Any luck with… figuring this all out?"

"Not yet." Angie stepped a little closer. "I'm gonna need to touch our friend trying to get into the fire. But I'm hesitant to."

"Can't blame you." No telling what she'd see when she did. "Sure you want to?"

"It'll cut to the chase. Your magic isn't breaking his compulsion to walk into the fire. Probably it should be, right?"

Oh. Yeah. Probably. Though not always. Her magic was weird that way. Sometimes it broke through spells to save people. Other times, not so much. Depended on what the spell was doing and whether the person wanted to be saved or not. If they wanted out of the spell, the Protector magic snapped that spell in half because, well, protecting. But if they'd *chosen* the spell for whatever reason, and were resistant to being protected from it, it didn't break.

This guy was resistant to being protected. He wanted into that fire.

And maybe he'd volunteered to be here. So there was only so much her Protector magic could do. People had to *want* to be protected for the full power of her magic to work.

Which in this case, was sort of a pain in the ass. If her magic had broken whatever trance or spell this guy was under, they could just ask him what was happening.

"So," Cary said, while Angie steeled herself to touch the man, "anyone got more than the goddess explanation? Like, why sacrifice into fire at Beltane? What's that about? Not really…Beltane-y, is it. Beltane's supposed to be all about, like, fertility and prosperity and that kind of thing, right? May poles and naked dancing and stuff?"

"This will provide our prosperity," the older woman said. "This is the only way to appease the goddess."

"Mmm." That didn't sound at all like the goddess of most neopagan and Wiccan traditions. But since Cary wasn't an active participant in those communities, maybe she'd missed a new development? "Can't just throw in something less…already living? Like a scarecrow or something made of paper machete?"

"She requires blood."

"Never understood that. Why a god would want blood sacrifice? I mean, I can see it with demons. All that fear and pain feeds them as well as the actual blood. And don't even get me started on vampires. Actually, vampires hate fire, though, so this wouldn't be something they'd be into. Just the blood. But demons…they'd be keen on someone roasting alive as a sacrifice. They like that sort of thing. Only they wouldn't be bothered with trances and spells that made the sacrifice unafraid to be…well, sacrificed. They like the fear leading up to it as much as everything else."

"We don't worship a demon," the woman said, her tone mild. "That is a common misconception among the uninitiated. The goddess is all that is love and goodness."

"That was my understanding prior to this night," Cary said. "I'm not saying your goddess is a demon." Although now that she'd said that out loud, the idea was not out in left field. It was possible for a demon to disguise themselves like a god, if it suited their fancy. But this set up didn't have the traditional markers of a demon summoning —no chalk circles, no demon summoning paraphernalia—so Cary wasn't so sure that's what they were looking at. "What I'm saying," she continued, "is that this seems more the kind of a thing a demon would like than the Wiccan goddess."

"She always needs sacrifice. Willing sacrifice. He's volunteered. He wants to live with the fire."

"I'm getting serious cult vibes here," Cary said in an aside to Angie while not taking her attention off the woman.

"Yup." Angie sounded distracted, though, so Cary let her do her thing.

Cary's skills involved standing stubbornly between good guys and bad guys, and talking a lot as they waited for the situation to resolve itself in some way. Those were her superpowers. Which, she did acknowledge, were a strange combination of superpowers. She'd have preferred teleportation, if she were being honest.

Angie's superpowers involved actual magic, so Cary would just stall and give her time to sort out the magic whys and wherefores of all this, and do what she did best. Stand here and keep everyone safe. And maybe talk until someone broke and admitted their nefarious plans.

"So," Cary said, "goddess is due sometime soon, is she?"

"She'll arrive any moment. She is awaiting her sacrifice so that she may bless us."

"Sure. Of course she is. And when she…arrives, what does she look like? Wouldn't want to miss her. You know. Shame to miss out on the chance to meet a goddess just because I didn't know what to look for, right?" She felt the man she held flinch as Angie gently set her hand on his bare arm.

"She is all that is glorious and awesome," the woman said. She didn't seem concerned with Angie touching the man doomed to be sacrificed. Or with Cary's stalling tactics. "She will show you the true way when she arrives. You will fall in love with her, too."

"No, I'm good. No need for a love match with a goddess."

She could do with a date at some point. But her life didn't leave her a lot of time for dating. Run out on a guy more than once—because the job of rescuing an innocent person called—and he tended to lose interest. How did superheroes date? Maybe that's why they either didn't or ended up dating other superheroes. They needed someone who understood the whole running-out-to-save-the-world stuff. Although Lois Lane wasn't a superhero. Well technically. Cary kind of thought Lois might be a superhero in her own way.

"The goddess will welcome you and embrace you," the woman assured, pulling Cary's attention back to the present. "You have no need to fear. No more need to worry."

"Definitely cult vibes," Cary murmured under her breath. But also, she was really curious who or what this "goddess" was. "How much longer will she be?" Cary asked the woman. "You know, night getting on, early day tomorrow. Wouldn't mind meeting her sooner rather than later. You know."

She wanted to ask Angie what she was picking up from the man, but also didn't want to disturb her, so she kept her attention on the older woman who seemed to speak for the group. Maybe a priestess, if this was a cult around a goddess?

"So, glorious and awesome looking goddess? What's that mean exactly? Is she…like a Fae and hard to look at? Maybe a little red in the skin? Built of fire, or…" Cary paused. She was looking for supernatural answers, but for all she knew, this was the doing of an ordinary human who'd been manipulating everyone.

Maybe even the woman in front of her.

"I probably should have asked this sooner," she said, her gaze narrowing. "Are you the one in charge? Why are you the one speaking?"

"I am her vessel. When she speaks, she speaks through me."

"Ah." Okay, so either they had a manipulative human situation. Or the woman was channeling another entity.

Cary shivered. Channeling reminded her of mediums channeling ghosts and she was terrified of ghosts and if this situation had something to do with ghosts, Angie was going to owe her several *bottles* of Tequila and not just wine. She'd need some of that too. But for ghosts, she'd require wine *and* the hard stuff.

"Do you…" She swallowed. "Do you channel the goddess? She enters you and you speak for her?"

"She enters us all. She is all of us at once. She will be him when he walks into the fire. Then we will all leap over the flames and be cleansed."

"All of you?" Uh. Wait. She'd assumed she was keeping this one guy safe from walking into his death—even if he was reluctant to let her save him. But now she'd have to stop fifty people from willingly risking their lives?

She glanced back at the fire. It had climbed so high now, she couldn't see the top of it from her angle at the base. That was much too high for jumping. And frankly, much too high for a natural, normal bonfire. They hadn't been feeding it this whole time. How the hell was it still getting bigger and bigger?

"Got a problem," Angie said.

"Yeah. Noticed. They're all gonna immolate."

3

---

*C*ary cursed under her breath as she watched the bonfire spark and grown taller. The scent of too many sweaty humans mixed with the scent of burning wood was starting to overwhelm her. Especially after just hearing the entire group intended on trying to jump over this fire that was now easily two stories high.

How was she going to stop them killing themselves on purpose? Her magic didn't work that way.

Cary wasn't really allowed to interfere with free choice. She could stop bad guys from doing bad things. And if people were doing things against their will—by drugs or manipulation or magic spells or something like that—she could stop them, even if they *thought* in the moment they wanted to do this dangerous thing.

But if they weren't under some sort of manipulative something or other… If they were choosing of their own free will to run into the fire and kill themselves, she wasn't entirely sure she could stop them.

This was a new twist in her job she hadn't had to confront before. Mostly, when she got in the way of good guys dying, they *wanted* to not die. They actively wanted her to protect them. Trying to stop a large group of people from doing something they wanted to do, even if what they wanted to do involved dying, was well outside her wheelhouse.

But… No. This felt wrong. Her Protector instincts had pushed her around the fire to get between the man and the flames. Her Protector instincts thought she needed to keep someone safe from something else. There was more going on here. Something or someone was manipulating these people into doing this stuff.

If there wasn't a "bad guy," metaphorical or literal, at work here, she wouldn't have survived stepping inside the bonfire herself. She wouldn't have been able to do that if her magic didn't know these people needed to be protected. Her powers were working. So she should be able to stop this disaster.

She could do with knowing why it was happening, though.

"Not talking about the mass suicide option," Angie said, her voice low, referring to her own comment that they had a problem. "This is a spell. But… I can't break it."

"Wait." Cary half turned her head to look at Angie, while still keeping her attention on the older woman doing all the talking for the group. "You can't break it? You've been trying?"

"It's… It's not that I'm not able to break the spell technically. It's that, if I do, it will…break them. This thing is wrapped around their heads and has been something infesting them for nearly a year. I can't just snap it this second without risking their mental well-being. I don't dare brute force it. And they aren't going to give me the time I need to weave through it for each one of them."

"Fuck. They're all bespelled. Individually? Not a group thing?"

"It's…complicated. A little of both? Best as I can tell."

"Can you tell *who* set the spell? A real goddess or something else?"

Angie was silent long enough, Cary finally looked away from the serenely smiling older woman and to stare over her shoulder at Angie. "What?"

Angie met her gaze.

"Not a real goddess," Angie said quietly. "But something…more difficult."

"What the hell is more difficult than a god?"

Couldn't be a demon. Cary had dealt with demons before and knew her Protector magic worked against them. Vampires, wizards, shifters… Same. Her magic worked on them all. But something more difficult than a god…?

To be fair, she'd only dealt with gods peripherally. Never stood up against one or had to defend anyone from them. And even then, her experience with gods was *very* limited. They rarely got involved with the day to day of humans. Which meant she actually had no idea if her magic worked against a god. And that was bad enough.

Something *more* powerful than a god…

No telling if she'd be able to protect all these people from something like that.

"An Elemental," Angie said. "An honest-to-goddess Elemental."

"Uhm…" Cary squinted as she looked at Angie. "I've only read about those, but I'm *certain* they do not involve themselves in human life." Elementals were…exactly what they sounded like. The elements. Earth, water, air, fire. They were…the cold wind blowing around the open field. The ground under her feet. The river they'd followed briefly getting here.

The flames at their backs.

Cary's gaze flicked up to the bonfire. The super huge bonfire that was growing without the addition of more fuel.

Elementals *were* the elements but they could also appear as incarnations. When they felt like it. They were more eternal than anything else on this planet. They couldn't be killed. They *were*. They would just continue on until the end of the planet itself.

That was…definitely worse than a god.

What the hell would an Elemental want with all these people? Why would it spend time weaving them into a spell? And…

"Elementals don't use magic," she said to Angie. "But you said there was a spell on all these people."

"The spell isn't the Elemental's. It's something else. But it's driven by and in service to an Elemental."

"Fire." She didn't even have to ask. The bonfire was *right there*. And the man she'd saved who was still leaning in the direction of the fire had been about to walk into those flames. They certainly weren't dealing with water.

Water might have been less scary. Well, no. No, drowning didn't sound particularly pleasant either. She wouldn't like to drown. Or get whipped up and pulled apart in a wind storm. Or sucked down into the earth. Yeah. None of the elements sounded like great ways to die. None of this sounded good at all.

"You're sure?" she asked Angie very quietly.

Angie nodded.

"Then…what do we do? Can't kill an Elemental. You can't break whatever the spell is without breaking the people. And my magic doesn't seem to be unraveling the spell because this guy is still leaning toward the flames." She tightened her grip on her erstwhile charge even as he made grabby hands for the fire. She shook her head. "You do not want to burn alive," she told him. "It will hurt and you will be very unhappy about making that decision when it's too late to stop."

"It will hurt good. I'll be cleansed."

She sighed. No talking to him when he was bespelled. But why the hell weren't her powers blocking this spell, breaking it, if it was so dangerous to him?

Because doing so would break him, she realized. The same reason Angie couldn't just brute force the spell away. Her powers could be subtle and delicate, but that took time, and usually there wasn't enough time for that kind of delicacy so brute force was the go-to. She could brute force her way through a lot of magic.

But that would hurt her charge. And the whole point of her magic was to protect her charges against all comers. Including, apparently, her own magic's tendency toward just muscling through.

"This is a lot more complicated than I thought it would be," she muttered.

"Yup," Angie said.

"Can you, with time, get through at least one of the spells? Like the one on this guy trying to immolate himself?"

"I can. But I'm serious when I said it'll take time. And in the meantime, there are fifty other people here who will be trying to jump *into* the bonfire themselves."

"She must have sacrifice?" the woman in charge said. "Our goddess demands blood, to cleanse us and heal us."

"Death is not the same thing as healing," Cary said. "It's just dead. And you can cleanse yourselves without all this." But she knew none of that was getting past whatever spell was woven into these people's brains.

Couldn't talk her way out of this one either.

"Magic isn't an Elemental's magic," she said, trying to work her way through what they knew. "So that means there's a magic wielder of some kind behind this, right?"

"Right," Angie said. "Helping the Elemental. And why the hell an Elemental would go to all this trouble, I have no idea. It shouldn't need to. Fire catches people out all the time, and people burn. But it's not necessary to an Elemental anyway. They don't need sacrifice or anything like that. They don't...care about sacrifice and stuff. They aren't driven by those sorts of motivations."

"Then even though there's an Elemental involved, somewhere around here..." She gave the fire a wary glance. "There's a magic wielder involved. I can work with that part at least." She wasn't sure she could do anything with or against an Elemental. But she could deal with a run-of-the-mill magic wielder. "We just need to find them."

"Far as I can tell, they aren't among the fifty people here." Angie narrowed her eyes. "But they'd want to see, wouldn't they? They'd want to be here."

"And get from the Elemental whatever it is they think they'll be getting from an Elemental in exchange for all this." *That* made a sort of sense to Cary at least.

Humans were forever making sacrifices to gods and demons and other powerful beings in exchange for...something. That was a real human go-to. Sacrifice something or someone and get something big in return. Supposedly. Didn't always work out. Especially with demons. They had loopholes in all their bargains and used them to kill the people trying to deal with them.

But it at least made sense, a human magic wielder offering sacrifice in exchange for something from an Elemental. Maybe the Elemental wasn't even involved-involved. Just here doing its thing and burning and not really noticing what it burned. And the magic wielder was hoping for some sort of return on all this sacrifice?

What would a magic wielder need from fire?

And why was all this happening on Beltane? Was the holiday a coincidence? An easy way to get all these people around a bonfire? Or was it significant?

"None of this is clearing up for me," Cary said. "Not sure what the point of it all is."

"Cleansing," the woman said. "We will be cleansed."

"Yes, yes," Cary said. "But you're saying that because you're bespelled. 'Cleansing' doesn't answer any of my questions. It's a generic reason. The kind of thing people say but that doesn't have any meaning. Unless, of course, you're going to take a shower. Then cleansing makes sense."

She wasn't really talking to the woman, more to herself, out loud, because she knew the woman wouldn't really understand any of this. As far as all these people were concerned, this made sense to them. They didn't see the nonsensicalness of it all and wouldn't just by listening to Cary ramble.

But it made her feel better to say this stuff out loud. Got it out of her system.

Whatever the Elemental was offering the magic wielder, or whatever the magic wielder thought they'd get from the Elemental, it had to be a lot if it required a fifty-person sacrifice. And stepping into a bonfire, instead of say, jumping over it, would definitely go against self-preservation instincts, so that would take a *lot* of magic manipulation to get people to go against their own survival instincts. Definitely the kind of thing that happened in cults, right? Well, she wasn't absolutely sure. Cults freaked her out, so she didn't study them. She wasn't afraid of them like she was ghosts. Ghosts terrified her. But cults were pretty high on her list of things she preferred to know as little about as possible.

Kind of regretted that at the moment.

The man she was holding gave another tug toward the fire. He wasn't struggling hard against her hold, and she was pretty sure that wasn't just because she was super strong—because she wasn't. Her magic might be. But she most certainly wasn't. His efforts to reach the fire were getting weaker the longer she held him in place.

"Hey," she said to him, turning her head slightly so she could see the side of his face. "You doing okay? Still want to walk into the flames?"

"Yes. So warm." But she saw his brow crease and he blinked a few times. "So…warm."

"Yeah, actually the warmth is nice on a cold night, but just that. Don't have to walk into a bonfire to get warm. We'll just stand right here and warm up, okay?"

He nodded, which surprised her, and relaxed into her almost fully, in a sort of resigned hug. "Right here is good. Right here is fine."

The woman's eyes widened, just a little, the first sign of an emotional reaction to all this. "He must walk into the fire. It's the only way to cleanse us all."

"Yeah, no. It's not. Really. Honest. It'll kill you. And I'm pretty sure you'd regret that later." She made a face. "Not that you'd know because you'd be dead. But I'm gonna ensure you live and then you won't have to regret anything."

The group, as a whole, as if they were somehow linked together and could coordinate their movements, all stepped forward.

Oh. That wasn't good.

"Get ready," Angie said.

"Eek," Cary said.

4

*B*ecause she couldn't let go of the man she was holding, even though he'd stopped struggling to reach the bonfire at her back, Cary couldn't move fast to get between the bonfire and the other gathered people. And those people were moving with a great deal of determination toward the fire. In unison. As a group.

All likely driven by the same compulsion.

And when she figured out who or what was driving that compulsion, she was going to have a lot of questions for them.

But before she could do that… "Here, take him." She handed the man over to her friend. "You can keep him from walking into the fire?"

"I can." Angie's voice was deeper now. "And with enough time, I can break his spell, I think. But I need time. You have the others?"

"Got 'em." Cary was *almost* certain her Protector magic would prevent them from walking into the flames. But then again, she'd never had to throw her borrowed magic up against something like an actual element before.

Angie wrapped her arms around the man, taking him into a hug that kept him securely in front of her and away from the dancing bonfire.

With her hands free, Cary took a few steps forward and placed herself firmly between the group and the fire. She even spread her hands out, a sort of physical gesture to let herself visualize the shield spreading far to either side of her. That wasn't strictly necessary. She didn't have to do anything but stand there. And no sneaking up behind her now either. Once she was in place, the persons she was protecting stayed protected, even from someone trying to do an end run.

But—and here was the tricky part—she wasn't sure who she was protecting in this case. Well, she knew. She was protecting the people trying to walk into the fire. Standing between them and the fire should work. But also, they *wanted* to walk into the fire—or at least were bespelled to think they wanted to—so she was weirdly protecting the bonfire from them?

No. Definitely the people. And definitely because they were bespelled the whole can't-prevent-their-free-will thing didn't apply. They were under duress. She could stop duress. Or something.

Anyway, this was a new set of circumstances for her powers and she wasn't entirely sure how it would work. So when the woman who'd been the spokesperson for the group hit up against her shield and stopped, Cary let out a breath. The others came up against her shield, too, and started feeling the air in front of them, as if touching an actual wall, hunting for a way through the barrier.

"So, my shield is working, at least for now," Cary said over her shoulder. "What now?"

"I'm digging into the spell on this guy," Angie murmured quietly. "Gonna take some concentration. You can handle them?"

"I've got this part." She hoped.

Not being in control of her magic, not being certain it would work in strange situations like this, always brought up her deepest fear. That she'd fail, that she wasn't good enough, and that her failure would lead to someone's death. She'd been a Protector just long enough to trust the magic worked most of the time. But every so often, she worried. Worried it wouldn't work the way she needed it to. Worried she couldn't channel it in just the right way.

Worried she'd get someone killed because she wasn't cut out to be a Protector.

She let those fears stew in her gut but didn't let them out in her voice or her body language. Angie had to concentrate. She'd be distracted if she thought Cary wasn't confident.

Cary took a moment to glance back at the raging flames. Was there something in there paying attention to all this? Did it care what was happening?

Was it just waiting for its sacrifice?

She watched the flames dance and sway, almost hypnotic in their crackling flow. If there was an entity in there looking back at her, she couldn't see them. Was that good or bad?

The people beyond her shield started to moan and cry. "We have to be cleansed." "We must step into the fire." "The fire will save us all."

Cary shook her head. Whoever had done this to these people, they'd really fucked up their thinking. She dragged her gaze from the flames and studied the field beyond the crowd of people. She and Angie had parked with a collection of other cars at one side of the field, and the rest of the open space had been clear of any other vehicles or people beyond the ones around the bonfire. But now, as Cary looked, she swore she saw some flashes of light from a copse of trees a few hundred yards away.

She squinted and watched those trees. Far enough they were mostly just shadows and darker blobs in the dark night. A moment passed. Two. Then...

Yes! There. A flash of light. White like a flashlight? No. No. She'd swear it was blue.

Blue like magic.

Witch or wizard? she wondered as she watched that spot. Whoever it was, she was certain that was the person, the magic wielder, responsible for all this. She'd been sure they'd want to be here. To see the culmination of their handy work. And on a dark night, those distant trees were a pretty good hiding spot.

So what were the flashes of magic light? Another spell? An attempt to break Cary's magic? Increasing the drive of the bespelled people to get to the fire?

Sweat trickled down Cary's temple, moving from her hairline

across her cheek. She swiped the sweat away with her fingers but didn't take her gaze off the trees.

She wanted to ask Angie about the brief but now obvious flashes of light, but she also didn't want to disrupt Angie's deep dive into the magic holding the man hostage to suicidal whims. So she kept her mouth shut and her attention on the spot in the trees where she knew the bad guy was.

And now that she had a bad guy, she had someone to put herself in front of.

But if she moved, if she put herself between the gathered people and the magic wielder, she'd also leave all those people free to walk into the bonfire.

Shit. Couldn't do that. And couldn't be in two places at once— between the magic wielder and the people *and* between the people and the bonfire. Not unless everyone wanted to get cooperative and the magic wielder placed themselves right next to the bonfire.

Cary didn't see that happening. If she got between the magic wielder and the people, would that even help with the compulsion spell? It hadn't seemed to help with the man she'd been holding. Or at least not quickly. That had taken time. She wasn't sure she'd have that kind of time if she moved away from blocking the fire.

Yeah, for the moment, she needed to stay between the people and the flames. She'd deal with the magic wielder in a minute.

She glanced away long enough to see how Angie was doing. Her eyes were closed, her head tilted close to the man's, her lips moving as she silently recited something. Cary caught a few of her hand gestures. That meant she was working a spell. Angie's spells required both words and hand gestures in combination for the spells to work. That and a judicious use of her actual magic. The fact that she was reciting a spell meant she'd likely uncovered something. Cary hoped she'd figured out a way to break the compulsion spell without breaking the man's brain.

If they could do that for one person, Cary might be able to give her the time she needed to do that for the others. But that would be tricky with the magic wielder just…right there in the distant trees. At some point, they'd realize what Angie was doing and come to stop it. Which…

Might not be so bad.

Cary liked to be able to look the bad guy in the face.

Still, she was itchy with the waiting. Wanting to help, to protect—it was her job after all!—but not sure what to do except stand there. Keeping people from going into the flames was the important part in that moment, but releasing them from the compulsion to go into the fire in the first place seemed equally important.

She kept her attention on the distant trees, watching and waiting. She knew it would be sooner rather than later. Unless the magic wielder intended on giving up and just going home.

That would probably be okay. She'd be irritated not to get a look at them. Not to know who they were and figure out what all this was about. She hated not knowing what something was about. That would definitely make her grumpy. But if they went away, that would give Angie plenty of time to work through the spell for all the people.

Still, Cary was curious enough, she kind of hoped whoever was over there would come out soon. She liked interrogating bad guys. Sometimes they even answered her questions!

The fact that she couldn't protect the gathered people *from* that bad guy yet, though, made her feel guilty about wanting to confront them.

Angie grunted behind her, and Cary leaned toward her friend without taking her gaze off the trees. "Everything okay?"

"Tricky bastard," Angie muttered. "Getting there. This shit is complicated. What the…" She fell silent again after another delightfully graphic curse.

Cary didn't ask anything more. Angie's response didn't answer her question fully, but now she knew for sure Angie was doing some witchy-break-the-spell thing and that was good.

What was less good was the way all the others in the field kept trying to push against Cary's shield to reach the fire. They were not happy about that barrier to self-immolation. There was some groaning, and whimpering. And Cary could swear she heard someone crying.

Crying that they weren't being allowed to jump *into* a fire? She shook her head. Whatever the magic wielder had done to these people, it was bad. And she was pretty pissed about that. And if she had any skills beyond defensive, she'd smack that person in the ass with a lightning bolt for causing all this suffering.

Even as she had that thought, she saw a little flash of light from the distant copse of trees. Brief, and bright. She had a moment to amuse herself thinking she'd somehow wished a lightning bolt on someone. Then Angie growled in triumph.

And someone stepped out of the trees.

5

"We're about to have company," Cary said over her shoulder as she watched the approaching person.

Her gaze jumped between the still-very-vulnerable people trying to scramble past Cary's shield to the roaring bonfire and the person likely responsible for that compulsion spell who was approaching.

The person, still too far away for Cary to see clearly yet, wasn't running toward them. Wasn't even jogging or walking fast. Just leisurely strolled in their direction through the open, empty field, over soft grass and uneven ground. Like they weren't in a hurry and had nothing to do later that night.

Maybe they didn't. Maybe their entire Beltane night was dedicated to this effort to make a large group of people jump into a bonfire.

A pretty sick way to spend a night, if you asked Cary.

Though, she really would like an explanation as to *why* all this was happening.

"Any luck with the spell?" Cary murmured, without looking back at Angie.

"I've got it!" Angie growled again in triumph. "Need one more minute."

"Okay, but whoever this is, they're gonna be able to get at the rest of the crowd soon. I can't be between the people and the fire and also between this approaching person and the people." She whispered this very last, because she didn't want her voice to carry.

The cold wind whipped through the field now, making the top of the huge bonfire dance behind her, sending out more sparks. The scent of woodsmoke swirled around them, a smell Cary usually loved. Less lovely now given the danger that fire represented.

What they could really do with was some rain. Her bad luck that in one of the rainiest parts of the country, they'd have to have a perfectly cloudless night of sparkling stars overhead and not a rain cloud to be seen.

Sometimes when Angie did big magic, nature burped and it rained. Maybe Angie could do that now?

Except Angie had a complicated spell to break. So no counting on rain.

The person Cary was pretty sure was behind all this was halfway across the field now, still looking unhurried. But they were close enough, Cary could see their hands moving together in a way that reminded her of how Angie did spells.

The bonfire rose higher. And the people in front of Cary started to scramble harder at her shield.

"Soon as I finish here," Angie said, her voice quiet and very deep now, "I'll set a protective circle at the base of the bonfire. That'll keep the people out of the flames, and you can get between them and the person responsible for all this."

"Excellent plan. Love it. When?"

"Soon. One more minute."

Since the bad guy was taking their sweet ass time, Cary *thought* they had that minute. She hoped. But she was bouncing on her toes in her desperation to get between that person and everyone else. Her Protector instincts were screaming at her to do that. And she very much agreed with her instincts. But if she jumped too soon, all these people would just walk themselves into the fire.

The approaching person's voice carried over the field now, reaching Cary on the wind. A mumbling of words that Cary couldn't really pick out as the person wasn't talking to her and was still too far away, but the cadence and rhythm definitely screamed spell to Cary.

Though, Cary was far from an expert on magic spells. Really, she was far from an expert on lots and lots of things. Unfortunately, some of those things were job-relevant and her more critical boss, Liruk, refused to accept the fact that Cary had not learned All The Things by now.

Cary often did regret not knowing All The Things. But there was just so *much*.

"Running out of time," she murmured. She hated to rush Angie, but… Yeah, they were running out of time.

She bounced in place, anxiety crawling through her gut. This was bad, this was bad. She needed to get between that person and the others.

The others, for their part, we not being cooperative. They insisted on desperately trying to reach the fire. So desperate they started throwing themselves against the solid but invisible wall of her shield and scratching at the ground like they might try to crawl under the barrier. Their cries and moans had turned into wailing screams, like they were already *on* fire and were rushing toward water. That part was wigging Cary out. What was being done to them?

"Need to move soon," she said to Angie. Because every Protector cell in her body was screaming, too. Screaming so loud Cary couldn't hear the voice of the approaching bad guy any more. All she heard was the screams and wails and desperation of the people in front of her, and the shouting of her own instincts to protect them.

"Circle is…" Angie's voice, very deep now. "Up. Go."

Cary didn't hesitate. She charged forward, already primed on her toes to move. Rushed past the screaming people as they fell forward, scrambled closer, some on their hands and knees, to get to the fire. She trusted Angie to make sure they didn't reach it.

She planted herself a good three feet past the group, but solidly in front of them and between them and the approaching magic wielder. And then just…stood there.

She was very good at just standing there when she was finally in place.

The magic that flowed through her to make the shields, the magic she got from her Fae bosses, wasn't something she ever felt. It just was. She had no idea really when her shield was up or when it wasn't by feel. She knew by the way things happened around her. The way bad guys couldn't get at the good guys. The way they got stopped in their tracks. But she couldn't feel the magic working, or the shield going up, or anything…

So when she stood still like this, when she had just a sliver of time to think before the shit hit the fan, there was always that moment, that brief second, when she worried this time wouldn't work. The shield wouldn't come up. And everyone behind her was about to get killed.

Fortunately, this was not the time when her shield failed.

The approaching magic wielder came up against the barrier of Cary's Protector magic with a little thump and a scowl that might have made Cary laugh if the person hadn't been trying to immolate a bunch of people.

"What the fuck?" they muttered.

Now that they were close enough, Cary got a good look at them. A woman of indistinct but youngish age. Maybe in her thirties? But could also be late twenties or even early forties. Cary was really crappy at assessing people's ages. She'd blame the fact that she often worked with otherworldly creatures and they could be hundreds of years old and look sort of middling age in human years. She'd lost all perspective on the whole age thing since becoming a Protector.

She conveniently ignored the fact that she'd always been bad at ages.

The woman wasn't an average looking woman, even if her age was impossible to pick out. Few inches shorter than Cary's five-foot-nine, she was curvy in that sort of overtly sexy way—all hips and butt and boobs with a tiny waist, which was a combination that baffled Cary when she encountered it in real life. The woman looked like someone had drawn unrealistic proportions onto a woman character in a comic and then the drawing had come to life. As far as Cary could tell, she wasn't wearing any undergarments to make that shape so extreme, but under the woman's gauzy white dress it was hard to tell. The dress skimmed over her tightly in a mermaid cut that showed off every curve, but the bottom of the dress floated in a flare of gauze over the rough ground.

Until she'd gotten close enough for Cary to study, though, Cary hadn't even realized she was wearing a dress. Either that was a weird trick of the night and only having a giant bonfire for light, or the woman was using magic to change her appearance. Either were possible.

She was a white woman with skin pale enough it caught the firelight and lit her in a kind of red-orangey glow that also painted her white dress in colors. Her very blond hair was pulled up high on her head in a sexy bun, giving her angular features a sort of sharp attractiveness that was arresting more than technically beautiful. And as she stood there, her dark eyes narrowed at Cary, some of that arresting presence made Cary want to duck her head and avoid the woman's gaze.

That was weird. To counter the reaction, she raised her chin and met the woman's gaze blatantly, with a small, polite smile on her face.

"Can we help you?" she asked, also with the veneer of fake politeness.

"You can get out of my way," the woman said, mimicking Cary's falsely polite tone. Her voice was rumbly but not particularly deep. There was resonance there, though, a sort of lilt to the higher pitch.

"No," Cary said, her smile widening. "Anything else?"

The woman's eyes narrowed slightly. "You're interfering in work I've been doing for several years. I won't have it stopped now."

"Shame. Since I'm stopping you. No people walking into the bonfire tonight."

"They're choosing to make the sacrifice. Willingly. You can't interfere."

"First of all, who says? Cause I'm standing here interfering. Second, I'm not sure being forced by a spell to do something against their own self-preservation instincts can be called 'willing.' Which brings us back to our first point. I'm gonna interfere with that."

"You can't. He won't allow it."

Oh man. Not someone *else*. She'd been hopeful they were facing the one bad guy.

A whispered memory of Angie's warnings about an Elemental went through Cary's mind. Shit. Yeah. There might be one of those back there at the bonfire. Could Angie's circle keep it contained?

"He who?" Cary asked, mostly to stall. She couldn't ask Angie questions right now, with the bad guy standing right in front of her like this, but she really wanted to ask if Angie was working on breaking the compulsion spell on the others and if her circle would hold an Elemental in.

Probably should have asked that last part earlier. Live and learn.

"He who's promised to be with me. Tonight. To give me the one thing I've been denied."

"Only one thing, huh?" She was half listening to the woman—who frankly sounded a lot like her own cult members even though they'd been under a compulsion, so what the hell?—and half listening to what Angie was doing. But she couldn't really hear Angie well, since she was standing a few yards in front of the crowd. She also kept hoping one of the people didn't decide to wander over to the very person who'd compelled them to walk into a giant fire because that would put them outside her protection.

She couldn't *force* them to stay behind her with her powers. And Angie had one circle up around the bonfire, but was busy trying to break a complicated spell on each individual person, so she wouldn't really have time to throw up another circle to keep the people in, or even pay attention to what each one was doing. Cary's only hope was that the ones who were still under the compulsion just kept trying to get at the fire—conveniently blocked by Angie's circle—and that they didn't realize they could turn around and go the other way.

Complicated and tricky situations really kinda sucked.

The magic wielder gestured down the length of her body with the sweep of her hand. "I am never denied anything."

"Ah. Okay. Cool?"

"Only one thing. Only one thing I want and can't have."

"Which would be?" Was Angie murmuring again? Or was that one of the people getting too close to leaving. Cary really wanted to look back and check on the situation behind her. She technically could. Now that she was protecting everyone, she didn't have to keep looking at the bad guy. But also, she didn't want to do anything that broke the momentary status quo that was keeping all those people safe.

"A baby," the woman said.

Snapping Cary's attention back to her.

"I want a baby. And I can't have one."

"Uh…" Well, Cary should have guessed. It was Beltane for fuck's sake. It was the time of year pagans looked for fertility! Hell, she'd even asked Angie about that part of the holiday. She should have guessed this would come down to *something* predictable like that. "What does getting a baby have to do with murdering like…fifty people?"

She was pretty sure that wasn't necessary at Beltane. She wasn't an expert, but human sacrifice wasn't one of the main components of the holiday as far as she remembered.

"Nothing else will work," the magic wielder said. "I've tried it all. I can't get pregnant by conventional means, and I don't want to adopt. I want a child of my own making. The Elemental will give me what I haven't been able to have any other way."

"Yeah, that's…" Cary shook her head. "That's a you thing. And frankly, I can't see how it would work." She raised a hand. "I don't want details because I don't need those images in my head. But what I do want to know is why killing fifty people is required?"

"How else to get Fire to grant me his favors than by feeding him."

"That's ew on so many levels. I just…" She made a face, gave herself a hard shiver. "So, here's the thing. We're not letting you kill fifty people just to get pregnant by a spark of fire or whatever." Still trying not to think about how that might happen. "Also, even the effort sounds suicidal."

"Which is why the sacrifices. He must be well fed before he comes to me. I want a baby, not to burn."

That was… Cary didn't want to say that made sense, because,

seriously, ew. But that was the first time the magic wielder sounded a little less like a fellow cult person and more like a reasonable person. And the fact that she sounded so reasonable when talking about murdering people was…bad. Yeah, that was bad.

"None of any of that is happening. You'll have to live with not having a baby in the conventional sense. It's fine. Lots of people don't have babies and are just fine. Happy even. Some even don't have babies on purpose." She was thinking about Angie specifically in that moment, but also about her little sister, who was on her second pregnancy and throwing up a lot, and how that didn't put any "hurry!" into Cary's biological clock.

"I'm not 'lots of people,'" the woman said. "I'm me. And I get what I want."

"Wow. Okay. Well. You're not spoiled at all, are you?" She rolled her eyes. "You know that doesn't make for good parenting, right? You won't get *anything* you want once you have a baby. Lot of late nights. Poop-filled diapers. No sleep. No autonomy. Lots of crying—baby and parents."

She was basing all this on her sister's experience because none of her best friends had kids. Some of her college friends and acquaintances did, but she didn't spend a lot of time with the people she knew from before she became a Protector—at least not the people who were strictly mundane. They either lived somewhere else, or were too ordinary and she didn't want them dragged into her new world, or they'd just lost touch and grown apart. Happened. And she'd consider that a bit sad later.

"I am prepared to do anything for my baby. Including anything I need to do to conceive one."

"Gonna have to come up with another alternative, then, because I'm not letting you murder a bunch of people."

"There is no other way. You don't think I've tried?"

"No idea. Not quite sure what level of stabby you are. Or well… burny? Is that a murder thing? Anyway, yeah, no. I have no idea if you've tried other things or not. I don't really care. I'm not letting you murder people."

"Not murder. They're volunteers."

Cary snorted. "Right. We've been this round. Don't play dumb like we don't both know what's happening."

She shrugged. "Semantics. They aren't being shoved bodily into the fire. The police won't call it murder."

"You think we're bringing mundane cops into this? I don't think so." Last thing she needed was more mundane people to protect. Especially ones who thought they could interfere and get in the way.

The woman waved her hand in the air, as if brushing the idea to one side. "Doesn't matter. I won't be stopped. Or caught. I will get what I want. No matter what I have to do. And there's nothing a little nobody like you can do about it."

Cary wanted to roll her eyes at the nobody comment, as if the magic wielder was "somebody." Well, Cary supposed she was technically. The somebody trying to murder fifty people. But really. That kind of talk always made her want to snort and sigh in exasperation all at once. "Nobody," she huffed. "What a load of crap."

"Out of my way," the woman said, some of her cool, calm exterior dropping. "I have an Elemental to fuck."

Wow. "I thought I told you not to give me any details. I really didn't want that image in my head. Plus, ouch. Seriously. The Elemental is *fire*. Ouch."

"That's why the dead people are necessary."

"Gross."

"Out. Of. My. Way."

Cary smiled. "No. Ha! See. There. You're not getting something else you want. If this happens enough, it'll get to be normal for you. You might even get used to it and stop with the, you know, homicidal tendencies."

"I get what I want."

"Not this time, sister." Cary was very tempted to make a big show of this and cross her arms over her chest and all that. Would serve the woman right. But instead, Cary just stood there.

As the magic wielder threw something at her.

6

Whatever the woman threw broke against Cary's shield, scattering its contents into the damp grass. The grass curled up on itself, not so much burning as just withering away until all that was left was a brown patch of dirt.

"Hm. Guess that would have hurt if it had hit me, huh?" she said. And looked up at the woman.

Whose expression of confused outrage was pretty satisfying.

"Out of my way!" The woman's scream filled the field, rising over the snapping crackle of the bonfire.

"No." Cary did finally cross her arms over her chest like an under-muscled bodyguard. She just couldn't resist. If the woman thought her spoiled murderous ass was more determined than Cary, she'd have another thought coming. Cary could out-stubborn anyone on the planet. That was her superpower. Stubbornness. Well, that and a carefully cultivated habit of talking the ear off, then pissing off, the bad guys until they went away.

The woman screamed again, looking around as if trying to find something else to throw. Was that her only trick? One bottle of deadly murder goo? Most of the bad guys Cary had encountered kept more than one backup up their sleeves.

"You really haven't been denied much in your life, have you?" Cary asked. "Coming with only one backup spell? That's some level of cocky confidence there. That's not a compliment, by the way. Per se. But really? Only one backup spell? Bet you didn't even think you'd need that, huh? Thought this would all go smoothly and you'd get exactly what you wanted without any issue." Cary shook her head. "You need to learn disappointment. It'll be good for you. A real learning moment this one."

She kept rambling, because she could tell it was pissing the woman off so much she was about to explode. Not literally—although that would have saved them all some trouble—but her blue eyes kept widening and the expression on her face got more and more enraged, and her pale skin turned a pretty startling shade of mottled red, and Cary knew the explosion of temper was coming sooner rather than later.

When it did, it was in the form of...the most ridiculous pout she'd ever seen an actual bad guy throw.

The woman threw herself onto the ground—literally *threw* herself onto the ground—and started beating her fists against the dirt while crying like the world was ending.

"Wow," Cary said. Again. This was...a lot.

She kept her arms crossed as she watched the meltdown. She might have felt a pang of sympathy for the woman if the woman wasn't trying to kill fifty people. "You really wanted a baby, huh?"

"Of course!" the woman snarled up at Cary. "It's what I'm made for. It's what I'm destined for."

"You know, you can be...destined for other things."

"I don't *want* other things. I want a baby. And not just any baby. I want an Elemental's baby. I want a god!"

Ah!

There it was. Cary nodded. Well. That was worse by a lot. But also made some of the weirdness slot more into place. And whatever sympathy she'd been developing for the pouting woman dissolved.

"Not just upset you can't get pregnant, then? You have to have a certain *kind* of baby. That's just rude, you know."

"What do you know? You don't have any idea. I'm *special*. I deserve a baby who's special too."

There was no talking to this woman. Cary shook her head and sighed. She finally figured she could look away and glanced back at Angie.

There were about fifteen people passed out in the grass behind her, another few on their knees shaking their heads. And Angie was steadily working her way through the people still trying to get through her circle to the bonfire.

So…that looked promising. Angie seemed to be able to break the spell faster now because as Cary watched, she went through another three people, leaving them to move on to the next person as they blinked at their surroundings and either passed out completely into the soft grass or collapsed to their knees in a crumpled pile of confusion.

Poor people. They were gonna need some therapy after this.

But at least they were alive.

The spoiled magic wielder screeched and Cary looked at her in time to see her racing forward, arms outstretched, her long-nailed hands reaching for Cary's throat.

She hit Cary's shield, hard, and bounced backward onto her ass.

"Serves you right," Cary said.

"Bitch," the woman hissed.

"To you? Yes. Yes, I am."

Cary really didn't understand the woman, any of this, at all. But she was particularly irritated that the woman seemed to think she *deserved* something so much she'd sacrifice all these people to get it.

Another flickering flare from the bonfire behind her made Cary look back again. The thing seemed to be growing. That was probably not good. No one had fed anything into it since she'd arrived. There couldn't be more fire without more fuel. Except there was. A lot more.

Did that mean the Elemental entity was doing that? The concept of the Elementals kind of confused her because they *were* and they were inside those elements all the time, but the…consciousness part of them, the thing that was an *entity* seemed to be maybe there and maybe not there all the time. The reading on them wasn't entirely clear so neither was Cary. And since this was the first time she'd encountered them in the field—or more precisely, encountered the idea of them in the field—she'd never tried to get unconfused about them.

Probably she should make a better effort. Liruk would tell her it was her fault for not knowing everything. Liruk, in this case, was right. But Cary would never admit that out loud to her.

"Fire's getting bigger," she said to Angie, in a moment when Angie was moving between two people.

"Noticed. Almost done."

She was, too, Cary realized. She was unsnarling the compulsion spell super fast now. Not just fast, but so fast there were only about five more people still scrambling at the edges of her circle trying to get to the fire. The rest were either passed out in the grass or sitting in the grass looking confused or standing staring at the fire but not making an effort to get too close to it.

So that was all good. But the magic-wielder currently pouting about not getting her way was still a threat because there was still a raging fire and a possible Elemental in there waiting for sacrifice. Which was terrifying.

Cary faced the woman again. She'd stopped trying to attack Cary—gave up fast, didn't she?—and was sitting in the grass in her sexy white gown just staring at the fire now, too.

"This is for the best," Cary said. "I'm not sure fucking a Fire Elemental is a good idea."

The woman glared up at her. "What do you know about anything? You think you've stopped me? I'll just try again. You can't keep stopping me."

Cary flattened her lips and tried not to reveal how exactly right that was. She couldn't follow the woman around, stopping her every time she tried something nefarious. They couldn't exactly call the cops on her—for what? The cops wouldn't have a clue how to deal with her. Plus, if any of the cops happened to like women, Cary had a feeling this particular woman knew how to manipulate that lust to her advantage. Bringing in a bunch of unprepared mundane humans to deal with her wouldn't work even a little bit. Might just give her more victims.

Maybe there was something Angie could do? Angie was from the "harm no other" school of witchcraft, as much as she was able, when it came to her magic. But Angie wasn't averse to using magic offensively, especially against bad guys. She'd done it more than once. The "harm no other" part didn't apply to bad guys *trying* to hurt other people. She might have a binding spell or something available?

Those were tricky, though. Cary knew Angie didn't like them or using them. The really good ones could bind up the witch casting them as much as it did the person they were trying to bind.

She was considering all the options for dealing with the spoiled magic-wielder when Angie came up behind her. "All done?"

"All done," Angie said, her voice very deep and rough. She sounded tired.

"Did you tap yourself out?" Cary faced her, frowning a little.

Angie was tall and thin, despite her quite healthy appetite, with a lovely, interesting face. People confused her for a model a lot because she was gorgeous and tall and skinny. But magic had always been her calling. And frankly, Cary didn't think Angie had the patience for being a model. Too much standing around waiting on other people. At the moment, though, Angie's face looked like she'd been sick for a few days and was a little more pale, a little too thin.

Cary wasn't sure she'd ever seen Angie sick. She definitely hadn't seen her this drained by magic work. Angie was a really really powerful witch. Seeing her so wane meant she'd had to use a lot of magic. Which…probably wasn't good.

"Not tapped out," Angie said with a tired smile. "I'm gonna need a gallon of nachos after this." Her favorite food and go to when tired. "And probably some Tequila. But I'm good. Recovering as we speak. Just… That was a lot of people and I had to work fast. Took a lot to do so much all at once."

"Bitch," the woman on the ground said, snarling at Angie this time. "I will make you pay for interfering. Your magic is nothing to mine."

"Bad guys say that kind of thing to you a lot," Cary observed. "It's so rarely true, but is it true in this case? Is she stronger than you?"

"No. She's good, though. But we're matched." Angie shrugged so casually it was as if they were talking about height or something and not magic that could be deadly. "No demons involved, so I'm good."

Demons? That…begged some questions. But later. Right now, "She's just going to keep doing this. And I can't be everywhere at once. She's trying to fuck a Fire Elemental and make a baby, by the way. Not sure if you heard that part."

"Didn't, but that makes sense."

"It does?" Cary's voice rose a little and her eyebrows went up near her hairline.

"Not sense sense, as in something an ordinary person might do. But sense in the way a person with delusions of grandeur might do something like this."

Cary frowned.

Angie shook her head. "Never mind. I'm too tired to make that make sense. The point is, yeah, I can see how this is all leading up to that. But…" She looked down at the woman still slumped on the ground having a pout. "It's not something that will actually work."

"It will," the woman spat. "I've got it all figured out. I did it once. I can do it again."

"Technically, you didn't do it once," Angie said, gesturing to the still very alive crowd. "And you won't be doing it again with these people."

"Who is sacrificed doesn't matter. Just how many."

"That's gross, by the way," Cary threw into the conversation. Because it was.

"You don't know anything," the woman said to Cary.

And wasn't the damned truth. Cary felt that way all the time.

"She's right, though, isn't she?" Cary said to Angie. "She can just keep trying this."

"I can put the word out about her in the witchy community. We can come up with a way to stop her."

"No, you can't," the woman said. "No one will stop me. I always get what I want."

Angie sighed. "She's a little spoiled, huh?"

"Yes," Cary agreed emphatically. "She even threw herself on the ground and pouted."

Angie shook her head. The woman glared harder.

Cary turned more into Angie and murmured, "But is there really anything you can do, or…?"

Angie met her gaze, and Cary could see she was mostly bluffing about getting the witchy community to stop the woman. "I can ensure she doesn't find any victims in this area ever again."

But what about…anywhere else? Maybe if Cary talked to her bosses. This seemed like it was something up their protective alley. In fact, she was a little surprised they hadn't tapped her for this. Fifty people was a lot to kill without it triggering one of their premonitions.

But then, working by premonitions and research and grunt work wasn't exactly a full proof science. Things got through, around, under. Stuff was missed all the time. If it was an exact process, nothing bad would ever happen again. But there was only so much her bosses could do.

Still, she could at least tell them. Maybe they could do…something.

She was still considering the impasse, when the bonfire flared again. So sharply upward many of the people behind Cary actually gasped. There were a few screams. And they all crowed away from the flames.

The magic wielder jumped to her feet, a sort of glee in her blue eyes.

That probably wasn't a good sign.

Cary had to put her hands out, and with Angie's help, keep the fifty pagans from stumbling in front of Cary in their hurry to get away from the fire.

When she was sure no one would trip outside her protection on accident, she said to Angie, "Is your circle…going to contain that?"

"It would," she said with a sigh. "If I'd designed it that way."

"Meaning?"

Angie cursed under her breath. "It's designed to keep people from reaching the fire, not to contain whatever is *in* the fire."

The woman cackled. An actual cackle. It was not a pretty sound. "You can't contain him. He comes for his sacrifices. He comes for me."

"Innuendo?" Cary asked. At the woman's frown, Cary said, "Comes…? You want to make a baby…?" She shook her head. "Never mind." To Angie, she said, "What do we do?"

"Move this now cooperative crowd behind you and you get between them and the bonfire and the woman at the same time?" Angie suggested.

"Good plan."

The magic wielder frowned at them, but didn't react to what they were doing for reasons that defied Cary's logical brain—probably because the woman didn't know what Protectors were, so didn't know what all the rearranging was about. Which was good. Most people didn't know Protectors were a thing. Safer for the Protectors that way.

Ironically, most people just assumed Cary was a witch, with really good shield spells.

With Angie's help and Cary's frantic hand waving gestures, they managed to get all the people behind Cary, and Cary positioned between all the people and both the fire and the magic wielder.

The woman who'd been the voice of the bespelled people moved up behind Cary and Angie. "What's going on? The last thing I remember, I was planning a rather ordinary Beltane celebration."

"Long story," Angie said. "But you were all going to walk into those flames and sacrifice yourselves for…" Angie shook her head. "For that woman to conceive a baby with an Elemental."

"What?" The woman looked from Angie, to Cary, to the magic wielder. "I don't even know who she is. That's all crazy. And I would not kill myself in a fire." She shivered.

"What's your name?" Cary asked her.

"Layla."

"Pretty," Cary said.

"Thank you," Layla said back with a soft smile.

"Layla, this is a long story that will require time and probably something alcoholic to drink while you're listening. Or you can pretend this was a weird night, and get on with your life never really knowing. Entirely up to you. But the explanations will have to wait."

Because at that moment, the bonfire flared so strongly it spread outward in a woosh, expanding toward them so fast, everyone gasped and moved backward a few yards in a hurry. Including Cary. Even though she knew the fire wouldn't hurt her while she was protecting everyone.

The only person who didn't move…

Was the magic wielder.

7

ary really hated protecting bad guys. It was one of the more irritating parts of her job. Sometimes it was necessary. Bad guys got themselves into trouble and sometimes needed protecting, too. But it went against the grain. Every time.

This was one of those times.

But it was her job. So she did it. Unfortunately, it could also be a complicated ask. Because she might, in any given situation, have good guys she was also trying to protect.

And this was another one of those times.

She couldn't leave the fifty odd people at her back unprotected. From either the fire or the magic wielder who'd started all this. But she couldn't just let the magic wielder be engulfed in flames from the rapidly—and unnaturally—expanding bonfire.

The flames rushed outward, shrank a little, the rushed forward again. Like a pulse. Like a heartbeat. And with every expansion, they got closer and closer to the magic wielder, who remained kneeling in the grass, her arms outstretched, her head thrown back, her ridiculously curvy body laid open and vulnerable to that rapidly approaching fire.

"Gotta help her," she muttered to Angie.

"Yeah," Angie said, sounding even less happy than Cary.

"You can keep everyone else at a safe distance? Keep them safe?"

"I can. But…"

At her hesitance, Cary glanced away from the expanding bonfire and to Angie. "What?"

"She's gonna do this again. And she will kill people next time. Maybe she should be allowed to…receive the consequences of her actions?"

"You don't sound sure about that."

"I'm not. I can't stand here and watch someone burn to death. Even if it's their own doing."

"Me neither. We'll deal with the rest after everyone's safe."

"She's going to resist."

"Yup."

"You sure?"

"I'm sure." Cary took a deep breath and looked at the bonfire again. "It's my job." Said with a great deal of resignation.

She left the fifty people in Angie's capable witch hands—so handy having someone powerful around who could protect the good guys too! That was not always the case for Cary in these situations—and ran forward to put herself between the magic wielder and the bonfire.

Which did not go over well. As Cary should have expected.

"Go away!" the woman screamed and grabbed at Cary. She could reach her this time, and she struck out with nails and hair pulling and all the stupid ways some people fought that were just vicious but also ridiculous.

"Stop that!" Cary snapped, attempting to grab the woman's hands to keep her from actually scratching Cary's face. "I'm trying to help you, you idiot."

"I don't *need* your help. You've done enough! But you've lost. I will get my baby. I will get my prize!"

"A baby isn't a prize. That's a gross thing to say." Cary tried to clamp both the woman's wrists together but the woman was slippery from sweat and her hands popped out of Cary's grip. Shit. This was one of those times she could use the super fighting skills her friend

Lucy was always trying to teach her but which Cary never had time to properly practice. "Babies are babies, not…trophies."

"My baby will be a glorious being of light. The perfect culmination of my life."

"Stop that," Cary said again, trying, unsuccessfully, to keep the woman from pulling at her ponytail. "Ouch. Listen, this isn't happening. Okay. Let it go. Go have a baby the ordinary way."

"I can't," the woman hissed. "Did you forget that?"

"No. But this isn't just about having a baby or you'd have come up with a less homicidal way of doing it. If you really wanted just a baby, you'd find that other way. You don't want a baby. Not really. You want a…a prize. And that's wrong. And I'm not letting you burn up in a bonfire because of wrong thinking. Even if that wrong thinking brought you here to kill people." Cary scowled. Everything she'd just said irritated her. Because it was true.

The woman pushed and shoved at Cary. And she was strong! Stronger than she looked. Cary tried to push back. She should have had some added strength and skills to stop the woman because of Protector magic. But… Nothing. Just her. Fighting ridiculously with a woman trying to burn herself alive.

Wait. No Protector magic help…

Shit. The woman didn't want protecting. Cary's powers, her magic, didn't seem to be working.

Panic nearly left her breathless. She needed her powers to work to keep this evil bitch from killing herself. But the evil bitch was determined to kill herself. Same conundrum as with the bespelled people. Except *they* were under duress and her powers had recognized that. She'd been able to stop them, despite their insistence on trying to immolate themselves.

Apparently, her powers weren't going to do the same for the magic wielder?

Damn it. She hated protecting bad guys, but she hated failing to protect people—even from themselves—even more.

"Stop!" Cary shouted, trying to get the woman to focus on her and stop fighting. "Listen. Listen! Stepping into that fire will kill you. I don't like you. I think you're wrong and probably evil. But I do not want you to burn alive. I do not want you to kill yourself."

"Why not if I'm evil?"

"I don't know. It's my job. And also, you're a living person and living people deserve to be saved. Even from their stupid selves. And maybe if you think about this for a day or two, you might be glad you didn't kill yourself." Having zero experience dealing with people trying to kill themselves was not helping Cary in that moment. Was she just making things worse? Was she saying horrible things or the right things? Would anything she say matter?

"I won't die," the woman said. She slapped at Cary's hands and put her face right in Cary's. "I will be reborn. And we will have our baby."

Then the woman shoved Cary, so hard, and so suddenly, Cary slipped in the damp grass.

Fuck! She went down, landing hard on her hip and elbow. Through the pain and momentarily inability to breathe, she had just enough panicked sense to roll and try to stand…

But she was too late.

The woman raced into the flames just as the flames raced toward her.

And Cary.

Cary rolled and scrambled on her hands and knees across the grass, hurrying to put distance between herself and the fire. She wasn't protecting anyone. She would burn, too.

She got far enough away not to catch any sparks in her clothes before looking back.

The woman stood, not burning, in the middle of the conflagration. Which was…a relief and not a relief all at the same time.

Her blond hair had escaped its updo and now swung freely in the fire's inner air currents. She held her hands high over hear head, her face turned upward, smiling as the fire danced around her, over her. But didn't burn her.

Okay. Well. That was…

Cary wasn't sure what to think. Good the woman hadn't just killed herself. Yet. But probably bad that the woman might have been right about the Elemental being inside the bonfire and there was about to be some weird sexy times. Cary was absolutely certain she didn't want to witness that. And she wasn't sure a supernatural baby was going to be in safe hands with this woman.

Angie hurried up behind her, helping her to her feet.

"Uhm," Cary said.

"Yup," Ange said.

"This is…"

"Uh huh."

"Should we…do something?" Cary stared as the woman spun in a slow circle inside the flames.

"What? I'm not going in after her."

"I'd probably get killed trying since she wants to be in there. And is…apparently not in danger."

"She didn't make the sacrifice, though," Angie said, her voice dropping to a whisper.

"Maybe she didn't need it? Maybe she just…wanted to kill a bunch of people?"

"Too complicated. Too messy. If she didn't need to sacrifice anyone to get her ultimate goal, she wouldn't have bothered. Those spells were complicated, took a lot of magic, and had been woven through those people over time. Lot of time. Like…maybe a year."

"And you broke them in minutes?" Cary said. "Well done."

"Thanks. Not my point. But…thanks. The point is, if she'd been able to get what she wanted without all that work, she wouldn't have done all that work. She doesn't strike me as the type to invest herself without something coming from it in the end."

"So…if she needed the sacrifices, and she didn't get the sacrifices, but she's still standing in the middle of all that fire… What does that mean?"

"I'm not sure. But I'm pretty sure it won't be good."

"Uhm…"

Cary and Angie watched as the flames began to shrink again, the giant bonfire which had grown to an absurd and dangerous size in the open field, slowly eased back to its original size. Still large, but not engulfing the area. To Cary's amazement, the grass that had *just* been underneath a roaring fire wasn't burned. It sprang back up like a hand had been run over it and nothing more.

As the flames shrank around her, the magic wielder followed, but her triumphant smile dimmed, fell away. She still wasn't getting burned by the flames, but they were receding from her fast enough she had to hurry to stay inside the bonfire.

"No," she said. "No! Don't leave me. Do you still want the sacrifices? I can get them. They're right here. All for you. You can take them. I will do whatever you want. Please!"

The fire continued to shrink. The woman found herself outside the flames and raced back into them.

Cary winced and gasped at the same time. Certain the woman was going to catch on fire at any moment. She still didn't. Despite moving in and out of the flames. Still. The sight was so disconcerting, Cary nearly bolted forward to try and save the woman again. She only didn't because Angie held her back with a hand on her arm.

"You'll burn," Angie warned. "She doesn't want protecting."

Angie was right. Cary hated it. But she was right.

Didn't make standing still while the woman kept running *into* the flames any easier.

"Please!" the woman begged. "I will do anything for you. Please."

"Is the fire…is the Elemental rejecting her?" Cary asked, quietly.

"Looks like. Not sure that's ever happened to her before," Angie said.

"She's not going to like that."

"Nope."

The woman's scream of outrage confirmed their prediction. "No! You can't leave me. You have to help me. You have to give me a baby. You *have* to!"

From the midst of the fire, something started to coalesce. Cary thought it might be a trick of the flickering light and seeing through it to a distant tree on the other side of the field. But as the coalescing got thicker, and formed more of a shape, she realized that was happening *inside* the bonfire. Not a tree in the background. A vague shape inside the fire taking form.

The shape was vaguely human, with a head, two legs, two arms. All of the shape was still made of flame. And there was no discernable gender to the shape. Nothing to say male or female or some combination of the two. Which probably wasn't exactly what the magic wielder had in mind. But then again, how did you get pregnant by something that *was* fire? Cary had some doubts about the anatomical possibilities of that—and really, she didn't want to think about it too closely. She was all for other people living their best lives and enjoying their own personal kinks, so long as everyone consented and didn't do any permanent damage to themselves. Just that fucking fire wasn't one of her particular kinks.

Still, this whole thing seemed so dangerous. The fact that the magic wielder was still standing in the middle of all that fire without getting burned though, did look…significant.

The shape continued to coalesce until there was a being a flame and solidity standing in the middle of the remaining bonfire, about a foot in front of the pouting magic wielder. She'd stopped screaming and demanding the fire make her pregnant and was now just staring at the entity. She seemed to sway side-to-side in a kind of imitation of the way the flames wavered, the way the entity wavered.

"Is that…?" Cary murmured to Angie.

"Yup."

Cary could swear she heard Angie gulp. That was bad. Angie didn't *gulp*.

"Do we… Should we do… Something?"

"What?" Angie said. "She still won't let you protect her."

True. Still. "Can you draw a circle around the bonfire again? To keep things *in* this time?"

"I don't want to piss off an Elemental," Angie said. "They can't die and can't be banished to a different realm like a demon, and I don't have any appropriate weapons to dissolve its corporeal form. So I really don't want a Fire pissed off at me."

"Fair. You think the circle might do that?"

"I think any movement that draws its attention to us would be bad."

"Ah. Yeah. Probably. Good point."

"You two are still talking," Layla said quietly from behind them. "Maybe don't even do that."

Cary nodded. She realized everyone around them, from the people sitting in the grass, to those who'd managed to get back to their feet, were all absolutely still. No one moved. Cary couldn't hear much in the way of breathing either. Though, to be fair, the sounds of the fire crackling filled the open field and probably would have covered the sounds of breathing even if anyone was. Which she wasn't entirely sure they were. Holding their breath was going to get uncomfortable soon. But she understood the impulse. She realized she was holding her breath too.

The vaguely human-shaped Fire entity stood about a foot taller than the woman, and gave the impression by the tilt of its head that it was looking down at her. She stared up at the head, which didn't have a face in it with eyes or mouth or anything, just the general shape of a head fully covered in flames.

Cary's pulse rate was through the roof—if there'd been a roof—as she watched the scene. She wanted to do something, to stop... Well, she wasn't sure what. Stop the woman from getting hurt. Stop anyone from getting hurt. But, like Angie, she was terrified of calling the Elemental's attention to her. Not that that would stop her getting between the woman and the Fire. Fear never stopped her running in and doing her job, which she recognized as maybe a character flaw. Still, she didn't immediate rush forward mostly because she was officially frozen in place. Good for protecting those already behind her. Not so good for protecting the woman inside the bonfire.

Who didn't want protecting anyway, so...

In the silent crackling of fire, a voice finally seemed to rise from the depths of the flames. "You are not worthy of what you ask," the voice said. "You will not be granted your request."

The woman wailed in denial. "Is it because I haven't provided sacrifice? That's not my fault." She pointed back at Cary and Angie. "It's their fault! They stopped me."

Cary scowled. "So much for staying innocuous and not drawing its attention," she muttered.

"But they're still here," the magic wielder went on, sounding placating now. "Your sacrifices. You can have them. I'll get them for you."

"No," Cary said firmly. Loudly. "That's not happening. No sacrificing. Sorry." The last said to the Fire with a little shrug. It may be a literal element, but she still wasn't letting the woman feed it living people. Not on her watch.

The Fire's head turned in her direction.

This time Cary gulped. She was a gulper, so this wasn't an unusual reaction for her.

But she did it with a lot of feeling.

8

espite the terrifying attention of a Fire Elemental being trained directly on her, Cary still moved a little forward so she was firmly between the people behind her and the bonfire. Even Angie remained safely behind her. With all those people to protect, Cary hoped her magic was enough to ward off the power of a literal element.

No breeze blew through the open field now. No one behind her moved or made any sounds. Just the crackling fire, the disconcertingly nice smell of burning pine, and the wave of heat from the flames. Sweat trickled down Cary's back under her leather jacket, but she didn't back down.

She stared at the entity that seemed to be staring at her. Hard to tell since it didn't have eyes. In her peripheral vision, she watched the woman—still not burning as she stood inside the flames—pointing at Cary.

"That's the one. She's the one who must die. She is preventing me from properly honoring you."

Cary sighed. "If honoring you means people have to die, then, yeah. Yeah, I'm going to prevent that. Again, sorry. Sort of. But..." She shrugged. "It's my job."

The Fire didn't comment. Just sort of wavered there amidst the flames. Part of it all and yet just solid enough to be a separate thing.

Cary waited for the hit of fire against her shield. For the bonfire to expand again. For…something.

But for a long time, nothing happened at all. The woman continued to babble to the Fire about being denied his sacrifices and he needed to kill Cary and everyone else and she was owed a baby and blah blah blah. Cary and the Fire continued to stare at each other. Although, was it really staring when one of the entities involved didn't technically seem to have eyes?

After what felt like a long long time based on the sheer amount of stuff the woman managed to say in the intervening period, the Fire finally said, "I require no sacrifice today."

Cary felt her shoulders droop a little before she straightened them again. There was still a "today" in that sentence. And the woman was still standing inside the bonfire.

"What exactly does that mean?" Cary asked, carefully. "I mean, great news. Seriously. Very happy to hear no sacrificing today. But… Uhm." She flicked a glance down at the woman. "She's still…eager for a baby." Cary raised a hand quickly. "I don't mean for her to get hurt, by the way. She's a bit on the evil side and all, but, yeah, don't burn her or anything. I know it's what you do, but it'd be really nice if maybe no one died tonight. Sort of a holiday present, right? It's Beltane. Good night for fire. Be a nice little present, no one getting killed. Right."

She pressed her lips together. Rambling was usually a superpower but she felt, even without Angie's reminder, that this was probably not the time.

"No sacrifices will ever be required," the Fire said. "We do not… want them."

That pause before want was interesting. Cary wasn't entirely sure what to make of it.

"There will be no sacrificing on this night." The Fire turned its head so it appeared to be looking down at the woman again. "I will take no sacrifice. Your request is not granted. Fire will not provide what you ask."

"No! You have to. You have to. It's the only way. Please! I've done everything! I've worked for months and months. You *have* to."

"We do not *have* to do anything," the Fire said.

Cary sort of wanted to gulp again and wave the woman to silence. That tone didn't sound good. Demanding something from an Elemental seemed dangerous. Not that the woman wasn't already playing with fire.

Cary rolled her eyes at herself. But really, she couldn't have resisted that phrasing.

"Please. I beg you," the woman said. She dropped to her knees and raised her arms in supplication. "Please. You must. I deserve this! I've earned it!"

"You are not worthy," the Fire said. "You are denied."

"No!" She continued to wail and scream and demand and talk.

And all Cary could think was, *Shut up already*! But she kept her own mouth tightly closed. Because the Fire turned its attention back to her while the woman babbled.

"You are worthy," the Fire said to her. Which finally stopped the stream of chatter from the woman. "I would grant you a request." Another interesting pause, then, "For the holiday."

Cary felt her stomach drop, that sort of roller coaster drop that could have been thrilling but in this case was more terrifying and definitely overrode her rational thinking for a split second. "Uhm."

Yeah, that was super eloquent.

She swallowed hard and tried again. "I really don't need anything. Really. I'm good. Only thing I want is for no one here to die tonight. No sacrificing. No people burned up. Just everyone walking away from this fine and healthy and all good."

She paused to consider her phrasing. Shit. Had she said something that could have unintended results? Was this like dealing with demons, where there were always loopholes and unexpected consequences and those consequences were bad? She couldn't see any potentially bad results from what she'd just said, but then she wasn't an Elemental. She had no idea how they thought about this sort of thing.

"Honestly," Cary said, "I don't need anything. Just want everyone to walk away from this still alive and healthy."

"Not everyone here is healthy," the Fire said.

"Wait. What?" She glanced behind her.

Layla looked between the bonfire and Cary, her eyes narrowed. "It can't know," Layla murmured quietly.

"Know what?" Cary asked.

"I have cancer. I'm in remission but… Yeah, I have cancer."

"I'm so sorry," Cary said, sincerely.

Layla waved that away. "It's fine. Well, I mean, it's not. But it's good for now. Remission gives me a chance. Time to really enjoy life, ensure I spend as much time as possible with the people I love. There's no telling how many years I have. Could be a full lifetime. It's just… you know, there. In the background."

Cary's anger flared suddenly. Not at the cancer news. That sucked, but it happened. Life sometimes sucked. But at the woman who'd almost robbed Layla of her time!

Cary glared at the woman. "You really are a bitch, you know that. A selfish, selfish bitch."

"Fuck you," the woman said.

Peevishly, Cary wanted to stick her tongue out at the woman. She didn't. Because she was supposedly a grown up. But it was super tempting.

"It is Beltane," the Fire said.

Which brought Cary's attention back to it. It was looking at her again. She raised her brows. "Yes. Yes, it is."

"I am celebrated at Beltane."

"Uh huh." Weird change of subject. But okay. So long as it didn't involve killing people, she was good.

"You have proven you are worthy," the Fire said to Cary.

"Thanks?" Not that she was trying to prove anything. Just keep everyone alive.

"I will grant your request. It is done."

"Uh, wait. Which request?" She hadn't made a request. Had she? Shit.

What had she requested? Was this like the old *Ghostbusters*, the first one where one of the characters who's not supposed to be thinking of anything accidentally thinks about that giant marshmallow guy and the marshmallow guy shows up to destroy New York City? She would remember thinking about a marshmallow guy. So it wasn't that. But...

What had she done?

The vaguely human shape of the Elemental dissolved back into the fire, so there was nothing distinct anymore. Just a lot of dancing flames. The magic wielder remained inside the flames. She'd returned to denial and begging and screaming, but Cary was so terrified of what was about to happen, she barely noticed. Noticed enough to know the woman was still not burning. But that was about it.

The bonfire started to pulse again, like it was breathing. In and out. The entire thing contracting and expanding in waves. And each expansion got larger. But rather than growing higher and just generally bigger, it pushed outward, then inward, then farther outward, in ever increasing rings. Cary realized that movement was turning it into a kind of donut shape, a ring of fire that kept getting progressively larger.

The movement and changing shape of the fire left the magic wielder outside the flames finally, which let Cary take a breath. But then the expanding ring got close enough for Cary to feel the heat as it brushed up against her shield.

And then the flames got closer.

Cary frowned. Her heartbeat hammered. Wait. That...

Was that going to...?

She'd barely thought the thought, when, with a sudden contraction, pulling the shape almost all the way back to the original bonfire size, the ring of fire shot outward.

And washed right over the top of Cary and everyone behind her.

9

Cary gasped as flames surrounded her, rushed past her, flowed over Angie and the other pagans who'd gathered for the Beltane festival. There were gasps, screams cut off abruptly, shouts.

But Cary was too shocked to scream. To stunned to move.

Her shield had failed. Her shield had failed. Everyone was going to burn because she'd failed.

How? What had happened? What had gone wrong? She couldn't think enough to answer those questions. The panic and overwhelming sense of failure took all her remaining brain cells. That and the knowledge that she was about to die.

Except…

The flames weren't burning her.

There was heat. Warmth. The crackling of fire in her ears. Everything around her seen through the dancing orange-red glow. She looked down at her hands. Her skin was glowing. Faintly, and hard to differentiate inside the fire, but there was a white glow along her skin. A few dancing sparks.

But she wasn't burning.

Did that mean her shield was working? But if so, why had the fire gotten past her? How had it gotten past her? If her shield was working, the fire should have gone around the group, not *through* it.

She turned to face the rest of the group. Only to realize no one else was burning either. Despite the gasps and screams and shouts. No one was *actually* on fire. Just standing or sitting in the middle of all those flames, the flames touching them and encompassing them, and yet nothing bad was happening.

As she stared, dumbfounded and too shocked to do more, she watched other people begin to glow slightly, their skin taking on a faint almost glittery look. The screams died down, replaced by a silence broken only by the still crackling sound of fire. A lot of glancing around. Looking at everyone else. Cary glanced at Angie, who's brows were raised high as she studied her hands.

She looked up at Cary. Cary winced. Angie shrugged.

Before Cary could regain enough brain cells to speak, and with a suddenness that was as shocking as the initial wash of fire, the fire sank into the soils.

And went out.

Plunging the field into darkness.

Cary stood in that absolute darkness for a long moment, listening to the utter silence, broken only by the sounds of distant traffic on the highway a few miles away. A few industrious crickets started singing after a few moments. And in the trees, a night bird hooted.

Blinking as her eyes adjusted to the dark, she turned in a slow circle.

No fire at all. Not even any dancing in the spot where the original bonfire had existed. Nothing. Just quiet, cool night. Getting colder by the moment. A residual sense of warmth in her skin. And the remaining scent of smoke and campfire lingering in the air.

She took a deep breath. Nothing hurt. That was good. She was pretty sure she hadn't burned alive. She faced Angie. Angie was staring at the spot the bonfire had been with a frown. She wasn't injured either, and her frown looked quizzical more than upset.

When she looked at Cary, she raised her brows in question. Cary shook her head. She wasn't sure either.

After a few more moments of silence, with her eyes adjusted to the dark night, she finally gathered enough brain cells to ask, "Everyone okay? Anyone hurt?"

A lot of murmured "no"s and quiet "fine"s followed by a whole lot of "what happened?"s and "what was that?"s.

Cary didn't have any answers for them.

Still frowning, Angie said to Layla, "Would you be okay with me touching you? I'm a touch psychic. I would be reading you. I won't without your permission."

Layla raised her brows.

From the crowd of people, a young woman stepped forward. "I see her all the time," the young woman said to Layla. "She's my psychic. This is Angie Jordan. She's really good. You can trust her." The woman looked at Angie, frowning a little. "I told you about the celebration. I invited you. But…I don't even remember getting here. The first thing I remember is seeing you and then the size of the fire behind you."

"Long story, Mabel," Angie said quietly. "We'll explain everything, I promise. But…" She turned to Layla. "Do I have your permission to touch you and read you?"

"What for?" Layla asked, understandably hesitant.

Cary was sort of curious about that question too, though. She sent Angie a little frowning question.

Angie said, "I have my suspicions about what just happened, what the Fire Elemental was saying. I just want to confirm."

"Wait, this is about…whatever request of mine it granted, right?" Cary said. "What did I do? Did I get anyone hurt?"

"I suspect it's the opposite," Angie said, still looking at Layla.

Layla's expression remained hesitant, but she stretched a hand out to Angie. Angie took hold of her hand, only that much, and kept a foot of space between them. She kept her hold loose too, so Layla could pull away at any point.

Angie closed her eyes, pulled in a deep breath, let it out slowly. When she opened her eyes, she smiled. A soft, genuine smile. "Well, Layla, you're no longer just in remission."

"What?"

"There's no cancer in your body. At all. Nothing. No cells I can sense that will flare to cancerous again. Anywhere. It was leukemia, right? I could…see the last few sessions, the drop into remission. But there's…nothing there now. I'd check with your oncologist. And a witch healer who can see deeper. Just to be sure. But it looks like the Fire healed you."

Cary blinked hard at Angie as Layla's eyes filled with tears.

"What?" Cary squeaked. "What?"

Angie faced her. Layla wobbled when Angie released her hand but before Cary could jump forward and catch her, the young woman who was Angie's client, Mabel, caught Layla and held her in a hug that involved a lot of tears.

"You said the only thing you wanted was for everyone to get through tonight and leave healthy and alive," Angie said. "The Fire brought up someone not being healthy—Layla that we know of. But if anyone else in this group had something…not healthy about them, I think the Fire healed them."

"Wait, it can do that? Fire can do that? Is that possible? How? What?" Cary could feel a low level of hysteria climbing up her throat as she rambled, so she shut her mouth, but her eyes were so wide they almost hurt.

"Listen, the Elementals are…not something I've dealt with before and hope to not deal with again. I don't really know what they can and can't do. They're a little scary."

"Yeah they are," Cary said with feeling.

"I thank them in my workings. I acknowledge them all the time. But meeting one incarnate like that is…" Angie shrugged, her eyes also widening. "I've seen some things. Some horrifying, terrifying, nightmare-inducing things. Things I don't ever want to face again." Her voice was quiet as she said the last. "I thought I'd seen it all, to be honest with you. But… This night was something."

"Something," Cary agreed. "Real?"

"Got me."

"But for now…" Cary looked around. "For now, it looks like all the Fire did was… Heal everyone?"

"Think so," Angie said.

"That's…"

"Yup."

Cary wasn't even sure how to feel. Since Layla was crying happy tears, and Angie's client Mabel was fine, and no one was dead and in danger of immediate death, she supposed she'd feel good. If super confused. And a little terrified.

The magic wielder who'd started all this remained in a heap on the ground a few feet away, where the fire had been. She was staring at the dirt, without much expression, looking beaten. Though Cary wasn't sure she was.

"Will you try this again?" Cary asked her without getting any closer.

"I was denied," she muttered. "I can't try again. That's not how it works. Once…once you're denied, once they *deny* you, none of them will aid you again." She glared hard at the grass. "You stole my one chance."

"Woman, you were going to kill fifty people. You don't deserve that chance."

"Which," Angie said, "is why the Fire apparently denied you."

"They require sacrifice! That's what everything I learned said. They require blood sacrifice!"

"Maybe just not the kind you thought," Angie suggested. She glanced at Cary. "You put your body and blood on the line to save everyone. Maybe that's what the sacrifice meant?"

"I was just doing my job, though," Cary squeaked.

Angie shrugged. "I don't know. They're Elementals. They don't think like we do. Maybe she just got a Fire whose concept of sacrifice was different to what she thought? I don't have a fucking clue. Demons are easier to understand."

"Demons?"

Angie waved a hand, as if dismissing that. "All I know is, we're alive and Layla's cancer is gone. And anyone else in that group with some sort of illness is likely cured, too. I'm gonna call that a win."

"Definitely a win. Big one." Cary looked down at the woman still on the ground, still staring at the dirt. She'd never even glanced at Cary, even when yelling at her. To Angie, she said, "You think she'll be an…issue? At some point? To someone?"

Angie shrugged. "Got me. For now? No. Not for a while anyway."

"I'm done," the woman said. "Done. No babies."

"There are other options," Cary said again.

"No. There aren't. No babies. No glory. No options."

"She doesn't really want a baby," Angie murmured quietly to Cary. "She wants the glory of birthing a supreme being of some kind."

Cary nodded. The situation still made her sad. But maybe it was best this way. She doubted this woman would be a very healthy mother given what she'd been willing to do here.

"I may…mention her to Jaxer," Cary whispered to Angie. "Just in case. Just…just in case." It wasn't so much that her faery mentor could *do* anything about the woman. But maybe put a word in with their bosses, and maybe everyone with the skills for it could just keep an eye on her in case she decided she might get a second chance.

"Do we just leave her?" Layla said, coming up close to Cary and Angie again. She was wiping the tears from her eyes. And Mabel still had a comforting arm around her shoulders.

"Can't call the cops on her," Cary said. "Charge her with what? Magic shenanigans? Attempted murder through magically induced suicide? The truth will get us all locked up."

"We could bind her magic," Layla suggested, this to Angie, and said very very quietly.

Angie shook her head. "You'll be linked to her. You'll be binding your own magic, too."

Layla had magic? Cary blinked. That was news. Maybe that's why she'd somehow ended up the speaker for the group?

"I would be willing to do that," Layla said, "to make sure she never hurt anyone else again."

"I can't make that choice for you," Angie said. "It's your choice, and your magic. But you've just been freed from one burden. Why take on another? Why not just be free for a little while?"

Layla shrugged. "My magic isn't doing me any good anyway. And I'm used to carrying the burden."

"I'd still council against it," Angie said. "But I leave the decision up to you. I'm not the one she tried to burn alive."

Layla nodded, her expression contemplative. "We'll see."

Which seemed to be her last comment on the subject.

It took the better part of an hour to get everyone organized, given enough of an explanation to satisfy their confusion, ensure they were all recovered enough to drive, and then getting the whole group back to their appropriate cars. Once Cary and Angie had ensured everyone else was safely on their way home, they did a circuit of the field to make sure there were no more unattended open flames remaining that might spark a wildfire, even though the grass and ground were still pretty damp.

And when they were satisfied everything was safe, they stopped beside the magic wielder again. Who was still kneeling in the grass and dirt near where the original bonfire had been. Cary stared down at her. Wondering what her name was. Wondering why she was like this. Wondering if she really wanted a baby this badly or was it an ego thing.

Knowing she had no intention of asking any of that.

She wanted to ask, again, if the woman would do anything murderous like this again. But she knew she'd just get the same answer she had earlier, so she kept that one to herself too.

As she looked down at the woman who still managed to look magnificent, even in her defeat, even with her once white gown caked in dark mud and her once perfect makeup dripping down her face, Cary sighed.

"Just don't do this again," she finally said. "You'll be stopped."

"By who?" The woman still didn't look up. "You?"

"Or someone very much like me," Cary said. "Enough. Find something better to do with your life."

"Fuck off," the woman said.

Another sigh. "Fine. Don't say I didn't warn you."

The woman's lip lifted in a snarl. Her only response.

Cary and Angie walked quietly back to Angie's car. Neither spoke until they had the doors closed and their seatbelts on.

"I need a drink," Cary muttered.

"We are in the middle of wine country," Angie noted.

"On a holiday," Cary said. "Well, not my holiday. But someone's holiday. Suppose there are other bonfires going on around here?"

"Goddess, I hope not. I'm done with bonfires for a while."

Cary snorted. Yeah, she was too. "Too late for any wine around here, anyway. But I have a couple bottles at home. We could sit up late drinking and telling the dogs about our night. And maybe make nachos."

Angie grinned. "Now that sounds like a good way to celebrate a holiday."

Celebrating, after successfully saving a whole lot of lives on Beltane, seemed like a good idea to Cary, too.

A good night in the end. Especially since the bad guy lost. The good guys won—and were healed! And no one died from the encounter with an actual Elemental.

But Cary was never going to look at a campfire the same way again.

THANK YOU

Thank you for reading A Very Cary Holiday! I can't decide if my favorite part is Fred being a beacon of hope, Lucy's Valentine's Day screed, or the way Tom really gets on Jaxer's nerves. All of the above maybe? At any rate, I hope you've enjoyed reading the stories as much as I enjoyed writing them.

If this is your first encounter with the Cary Redmond world, don't miss the first book in her main series, The Trouble with Black Cats and Demons. And if you'd like to read more Cary short stories, almost all of them have been put into collections at this point, staring with When Cary Met the Good Guys.

For those readers interested in Cary's witch friend Angie Jordan, she has her own series. The Demon Witch series delves into some of Angie's mysterious demon history, and you get a glimpse into why she doesn't appear to date much.

To stay up-to-date on my releases, sales, news, and to get a free Cary Redmond novella (which isn't available anywhere else), please join my newsletter at https://bit.ly/KatSimonsNewsletter. You can also find updates at my website, follow my author page at BookBub, or follow my author page at any of your favorite vendors.

Thanks again for reading!

KAT'S NEWSLETTER

Don't miss the latest Kat Simons

news, updates, excerpts, cover reveals, and more!

All new subscribers get two free stories.

∽

When Cary Met Ariel

A Cary Redmond Urban Fantasy novella

And

Mate Run

A Tiger Shifters Paranormal Romance short story

∽

***Join Now*!**

https://bit.ly/KatSimonsNewsletter

BOOKS BY KAT SIMONS

The Cary Redmond Series

* The Trouble Black Cats and Demons * The Trouble with Ghouls and Serial Killers * The Trouble with Leopard Queens and Shifter Wars * The Trouble with Baby Gods and Vampires * The Trouble with Magic and Faery Curses * The Trouble with Wizards and Old Enemies * The Trouble with Death and Demon Gods

The Cary Redmond Series Box Set Books 1-3

Cary Redmond Short Stories

* When Cary Met Jaxer * When Cary Met Pickles * When Cary Met Marianne * When Cary Met Lucy * When Cary Met Angie * Cary and Deacon (Try to) Go on a Date * Date Night Take Two * Third Date's the Charm * Cary vs the Goblin King * Dinner with the Joneses * Cary and the Cursed Jack-O'-Lantern * Cary and the Demon Witch * Cary Goes to Hawaii * Cary Holidays * Cary and Dragons and Goblins * Cary's Galentine's Day * Cary at the Haunt and Howl * Cary's Leprechaun Troubles

When Cary Met the Good Guys (Collection 1)

Dates, Dinners, and Other Disasters (Collection 2)

Witches and Weavers and Ghosts, Oh Boy (Collection 3)

A Very Cary Holiday (Collection 4)

Demon Witch Series

Howling Dreadful

Moonlit Strange

Bone Lantern Witch

Spiderweb Witch

The Seven Families Series

Wolf Family

Darkness in Stone

Redemption in Stone

Fated in Stone

Tiger Shifters Series

* Once Upon a Tiger * Along Came a Tiger * Here There Be Tigers * Her Tiger To Take * To Tempt a Tiger * Down Will Come Tiger * To Catch a Tiger * What a Tiger Wants * Taming Her Tiger

Tiger Shifters Series Vol 1 (Books 1 - 3)

Tiger Shifters Series Vol 2 (Books 4 - 6)

Romancing the Leopard: A Tiger Shifters-Cary Redmond Crossover Novel

Joan of Kerry Series

Joan of Kerry: Joan and the Abhartach

Joan and the Leprechaun

Joan and the Kraken

Haunts and Howls Collections

Haunts and Howls and Guardian Spells

Haunts and Howls Where Demons Dwell

*Tombstone Wizard * The Unshattered Sword * Destiny Through the Cats Eyes * Going Out of Business: Everything's for Sale

ABOUT THE AUTHOR

Kat Simons earned her Ph.D. in animal behavior, working with animals as diverse as dolphins and deer. She brought her experience and knowledge of biology to her paranormal romance and urban fantasy fiction, where she delights in taking nature and turning it on its ear. She writes urban fantasy, contemporary fantasy, and paranormal romance in series which combine action adventure, the otherworldly, and a frequent dose of sexy romance.

The latest book in her bestselling romantic urban fantasy series about Protector Cary Redmond, The Trouble with Death and Demon Gods, is also out now. As are the newest stories in the romantic urban fantasy Demon Witch series, including the first "meet cute" for Angie and her demon hunter boyfriend Sebastian in the novella *Howling Dreadful*.

The novel Darkness in Stone launches the newest paranormal romance series for Kat, following the exploits and loves of the Seven Families of monster hunters. The first trilogy follows the Wolf Family, as our heroes and heroines struggle to win their fated mates while fending off deadly monsters bent on destroying the world.

For something a little different, Kat also publishes fantasy, science fiction, and the occasional hockey romance under the name Isabo Kelly (https://www.isabokelly.com).

After traveling the world, living in places like Hawaii, Germany, and Ireland, Kat now lives in New York City with her family and a library's worth of books.

For more on Kat and her future books

Website: https://www.katsimons.com
Newsletter: https://bit.ly/KatSimonsNewsletter

Kat Simons Bookstore
https://tanddpublishingbookstore.com/

Social Media
Facebook Page: https://www.facebook.com/KatSimonsAuthor
BookBub: https://www.bookbub.com/authors/kat-simons
Instagram: https://www.instagram.com/isabokelly/
Twitter: https://twitter.com/IsaboKelly

www.ingramcontent.com/pod-product-compliance
Lightning Source LLC
Chambersburg PA
CBHW051303210726
48287CB00002B/638